NORTHERN D'LIGHTS

Another hilarious account of
"Growing Up North"

by Jerry Harju

NORTHERN D'LIGHTS

Another hilarious account of
"Growing Up North"

by Jerry Harju

Illustrations by
Rick Humphrey

Copyright 1994
by Jerry Harju
and Avery Color Studios

Published by Avery Color Studios
Marquette, Michigan 49855

ISBN 0-932212-81-6
Library of Congress Card No. 94-072584

October, 1994
July, 1995

Introduction

It's a pleasure to introduce my second book, *Northern D'Lights*. Like the first book, *Northern Reflections*, it's a collection of humorous short stories about the rigors of growing up in the Upper Peninsula of Michigan (correction—two stories are about WWII years in Milwaukee) in the 1940's. To me, even now, the Upper Peninsula is a strange, wonderful, and somewhat uncivilized place, but when I think back to prehistoric times, when I was a kid, it was even more so. What I've done in this book is create fictionalized versions of things that happened to me and characters I met during that time. I hope you enjoy them.

In May 1993 I retired from The Aerospace Corporation to pursue a second career of writing, and let me tell you—the writing business is a lot harder than the aerospace business. I am busier and more challenged now than I've ever been in my life.

One of the greatest satisfactions in writing books is meeting new people. During the past year since my first book came out, I've had a marvelous time signing books in book stores and gift shops around Michigan and Wisconsin. I've shot the bull with a lot of wonderful folks who have told me very funny things that happened to them when they were kids. But I just want to say one thing to all the budding humorists who have shaken my hand, cackled insanely, and said, "Har-ju? I'm fine, how-are-*you*?" I've heard it before—I'll hear it again.

I really like hearing from readers. If you want to drop me a line and let me know what you thought of the book (good or bad), I would appreciate it.

Jerry Harju
14002 Palawan Way, PH6
Marina del Rey, California 90292

Dedication

To my sweetheart, Pat.

Acknowledgements

Several people put in time and energy to make this book a reality. I thank my sweetheart, best friend, and editor, Pat Green, who read these stories so many times that she can almost recite them by heart. We finally had to quit improving them because they got so funny we couldn't stand it anymore. I thank Rick Humphrey, whose delightful, zany illustrations added immeasurably to the quality of the book. I also thank Jeff (a.k.a. Kippy) Jacobs, my partner in kid crimes, Chris, Cam, Roger, Mike, Harriet, and others who reviewed the story rough drafts and helped me get the final kinks out of them.

Table of Contents

Rest in Peace, Elsie Runkkinen

I'd never laid eyes on a dead body, and I could have easily gone a lot longer without seeing one, except for Kippy Jacobs. Kippy, my pal and partner in kid crimes who lived across the railroad tracks, had gone to his Aunt Beaulah's funeral back in June and for weeks afterward wouldn't shut up about it. "I jus' walked up to the casket an' put my hand on hers...it was cold an' hard—like a rock. I wuz gonna lean over an' kiss her on the cheek, but my ma pulled me away." With a casual, self-satisfied smirk, he then added, "It wuzn't so much though...if ya gotta strong stomach...heh, heh, heh..."

So when my mother asked me if I wanted to go to Elsie Runkkinen's funeral, it wasn't just a funeral, it was a test of guts. I hadn't joined the Boy Scouts because the old man had found out how much the uniforms cost, but if I had, I was about to earn my dead-body merit badge.

1941—a muggy August afternoon—the air still and heavy with the promise of a typical tooth-rattling Michigan thunderstorm. Blue-bottomed house flies buzzed frantically against the panes of my bedroom window as I sat patiently on the bed waiting for my mother to finish tying my necktie. The iron-hard, freshly starched collar of my dress shirt gnawed on my neck as she cinched up the tie.

"Keep your suit coat on until you've looked at Mrs. Runkkinen in the coffin, and then you can take it off and put it on the bed where all the coats will be. Don't forget and leave it there, though."

"Am I supposed to touch her hand or somethin' when I go up to th'coffin?"

1

"You don't have to touch her. Just look at her awhile, and then you can get something to eat. And don't get wild and start running around. Remember—this is a funeral. Pop and I will be there as soon as I finish baking the oatmeal cookies."

"Kin I have some coffee if they ask me?"

"No coffee—you're too young—I told you that."

Someday, soon I hoped, I'd earn my coffee merit badge.

She brushed the shoulders of my suit coat. "And don't forget to go up to Jalmer Runkkinen and tell him you're sorry."

"Sorry 'bout what?"

"That his mother is dead, numbskull—what do you think?"

"Oh."

I had a lot to learn about death.

The huge Runkkinen clan were crammed into an old wood-frame house down the street from us in Ishpeming, Michigan. Actually, *everybody* in south Ishpeming lived in old wood-frame houses. The Runkkinen household consisted of Jalmer and Lillian, their seven kids, and Jalmer's mother, Elsie, who had passed away in her sleep a couple of nights ago at the age of seventy-eight.

Jalmer hadn't landed a steady job since he'd been laid off at the iron mine in 1938, so times were very tough for the Runkkinens, and the funeral promised to be a no-frills affair. Hiring a mortician was a luxury that only rich people on the north end of town could afford, so Elsie was going to be laid out in her natural, unembalmed state in a wooden coffin made by a neighbor, Vilho Mattila.

I timidly shuffled into the Runkkinen yard which had totally surrendered to Jalmer and Lillian's battalion of kids. Except for clumps of quack grass along the fence, the lawn had long since been ground down to a five-o'clock stubble. A one-legged Raggedy Ann doll, a victim of the on-going kid war, sat in a well-dented, red Radio Flyer wagon by the kitchen stoop. Trudging up the steps to the kitchen door, I was assaulted by a torrid blast of air radiating from the wood stove inside. Lillian Runkkinen opened the screen door and let me into the kitchen. Lillian was a large, raw-boned woman with a florid complexion; years of child bearing and poverty had etched premature lines in her face. While trying to look her best wearing a new dress, she was rapidly wilting from the stove heat. She brushed a damp hank of hair from her forehead and gave me a watery smile.

"You're early, aren'cha? Your ma an' pa comin'?"

"Yeah, but my ma's still bakin' th'cookies."

"Well, c'mon in. You look real nice in your suit."

The sweltering kitchen was bustling with Runkkinen women preparing a mind-boggling assortment of food for the funeral guests. Three rhubarb pies sat cooling on the oilcloth-covered kitchen table. Emily, the oldest Runkkinen girl, was busily jamming large chunks of fat-laced ham into the meat grinder for the ham-salad sandwiches. Olga, one of Jalmer's sisters, was pulling a large cookie sheet of fragrant prune tarts out of the oven.

Lillian took me by the elbow and pushed me through the kitchen. "Why don't you go an' pay your respects to Elsie."

The dining room was taken up with a long industrial-sized table needed for feeding the Runkkinen horde. Huge pitchers of lemonade with large, floating chunks of ice sweated on the threadbare, white tablecloth. A couple dozen mismatched, chipped coffee cups were lined up on one end of the table.

By the far wall of the living room, surrounded by flowers and resting on two sawhorses draped with a dark cloth, was the open coffin. Elsie Runkkinen, eyes closed and hands folded across her midsection, lay inside. I took a deep, ragged breath and walked up.

Actually, she looked much better than the last time I'd seen her. She even looked better than Lillian, or for that matter, the rest of the Runkkinen women. None were raving beauties, but then they never wore lipstick and rouge like Elsie was now wearing.

My mother had said I didn't have to touch Elsie, but if I was going to match Kippy's funeral story, I didn't have much choice. I looked around. Lillian had gone back into the kitchen, so I was alone with Elsie. My right hand crept up, then quickly darted out—I poked her hand with my forefinger.

Gawd—it was like ice! Impulsively, I poked again—and a third time.

"If yer tryin' t'wake her up, yer a li'l late."

I shot up four feet into the air, whipping my head around. Clyde Runkkinen, Jalmer's youngest boy, had silently slipped into the room. His slightly crossed eyes peered out from beneath a dirty, ragged helmet of hair. Runkkinen kids were always easy to spot because Jalmer gave them all the same haircut—boys and girls alike. Rumor had it that Jalmer put a bowl on their heads when he cut hair, but nobody knew that for sure.

Eight-year-old Clyde was the same age as I was; however, among second-graders he was already known and feared for his macabre sense of humor. On the last day of school in June, when there wasn't time left for punishment by the teacher, Clyde had slipped a "chipmunk sandwich" into Martha Koski's lunch box during recess. A chipmunk sandwich consisted of a dead chipmunk between two pieces of white bread, with mayonnaise added for flavor. I imagined that funerals were right up his alley.

I quickly stashed my forefinger in my pants pocket. "Boy, dead people sure are cold, hey?"

Clyde looked toward the kitchen, then leaning over, said in a hoarse whisper. "You'd be cold, too, if ya spent all las' night layin' on eight blocks a ice in the woodshed."

"What?"

"Tha's right. My old man got eight blocks from th'iceman yesterday—wrapped 'er up inna bed sheet an' laid 'er right on top. Can't have 'er goin' bad 'fore th'funeral's over—heh, heh, heh."

Transfixed, I stared at the big chunks of ice floating in the lemonade pitchers.

Sensing that he had a captive audience, Clyde pressed on. "Not only that, when they went t'get 'er ready this mornin', the bed sheet had froze to 'er rear end. Ripped half the skin off 'er bum before they got it loose. But she's gonna thaw out inna hurry 'cause it's so hot. Betcha by the time they get ready t'take 'er to th'cemetery, she'll be gettin' pretty ripe. Stick aroun' an' you'll see what I mean." With another obscene chuckle, Clyde sauntered into the kitchen to filch a prune tart.

Lillian came out, wiping her hands on her apron. "You keep lookin' at that lemonade—would'ja like a glass?"

I shrank back. "No...no...I'm not thirsty right now."

Once Elsie Runkkinen's relatives started to arrive, the house was packed to the rafters in no time at all. Axel and Ida, Elsie's nephew and his

I stared at the chunks of ice floating in the lemonade pitchers.

wife, came from Bruce Crossing with three prime specimens of Ida's specialty—blueberry pies. Jalmer's younger sister Tyyne came from Trout Creek with three dozen prune tarts and got really peeved when she found out that Olga had also made tarts. Sharp words were exchanged in the kitchen before Lillian assured Tyyne and Olga that they were both expert bakers and that all five dozen tarts would undoubtedly get eaten.

The dining room table was now buckling under the strain of prune tarts, pies, cakes, and other assorted pastries. As more and more people drifted in, the temperature in the house inched steadily upward.

Most of the kids went outside to finish off the grass in the yard, but Clyde had planted a seed of grisly curiosity in my mind, and I hovered around the coffin, occasionally testing the air with my nose. All I picked up, however, was the heavy, sweet scent of the flowers combined with the sharp, resinous odor of the freshly varnished wooden coffin.

I didn't know anything about coffins, so this one looked pretty spiffy to me. It had a sleek, plain design with flat sides flaring up toward the opening and side-mounted dowels for pall-bearer handles. The walnut varnish gave it a dark, quiet tone. All in all, it looked like a nice piece of work, as only a skilled Finnish carpenter like Vilho Mattila could build.

This opinion wasn't shared by some of the men, however. A couple of the Runkkinens were good carpenters, and the others weren't at all bashful about talking about good carpentry.

Two of Jalmer's cousins, Muzza and Blackie, stood at the coffin, giving it a critical eye.

"Ya call that a coffin?" Muzza said. "He made it outta *pine*. Who makes coffins outta pine? Ya gotta use oak—cost a li'l more maybe, but a good oak coffin'll last ya maybe ten, fifteen years in th'ground. This one'll be fallin' apart in five years."

Blackie jabbed a finger at a corner about four inches from Elsie's head. "Look at this miter joint he made here—not tight at all. I kin see space between th'boards." Blackie then stuck his hand inside the coffin, his sleeve brushing Elsie's hair while he probed the inside of the corner with his fingers. "Muzza...feel this. He only used one-by-one-inch stock fer th'corner braces. What kind'a work izzat? I tell ya, I should'a made this thing m'self."

"Yer right," Muzza said. Then turning to Lillian who was feverishly pouring coffee in the dining room, he added, "Lillian, how come ya didn't have Blackie here make th'coffin, eh? He's th'best carpenter in th'family."

"'Cuz Blackie didn't get here from Calumet till an hour ago, that's why!" Lillian was getting a trifle testy as the funeral progressed.

A sharp gasp came from the second floor staircase. Violet, the second-oldest Runkkinen daughter, had come halfway down and was staring bug-eyed at Elsie.

Jeez, I thought, girls just can't handle seeing dead bodies like boys.

Violet ran down the stairs, bent over the coffin, and stared unbelievingly at Elsie.

"My dress...*she's wearing my good dress.* WHY'S GRANDMA WEARING MY GOOD DRESS?"

A hush came over the living room, and Lillian quickly put down the coffee pot and hurried over to Violet, putting an arm around her.

"Look, sweetheart...your grandma didn't have any nice dresses at all, an' she's about your size, so pa an' I figured you wouldn't mind..."

"I WUZ GONNA WEAR THAT DRESS TO THE LABOR DAY PICNIC...!"

"I know, I know, an' you still can. We weren't gonna bury her in the dress. It's just fer the funeral."

"You jus' gonna bury her in her underwear?"

Lillian gazed around nervously at the onlookers. "Uh...no...no...we'll bury her in somethin' else..."

"You expect me t'wear that dress to the Labor Day picnic after it's been on...on a dead body? No, thank you! You might as well bury her in it!" Violet turned around and ran back up the stairs.

"I wouldn't bury a nice dress like that in this flimsy coffin." Muzza said.

Lillian's face turned a violent shade of red. She stepped over to Muzza and spoke in a quiet, level voice. "Muzza, if I hafta kill you 'cuz you didn' shut yer yap about that coffin, that's OK cause we gotta 'nough food here fer two funerals. Now, you wanna go over an' tell Blackie how you want *your* coffin made?"

Reverend Karppinen patted his damp forehead with a white handkerchief. "I'm sure I don't have to remind you good people that for fifty-seven years, ever since she came over from Finland as a young woman, Elsie

Runkkinen, mother of eight children, has been a true inspiration to the congregation of the Bethany Lutheran Church..."

Karppinen's eulogy droned on in the oppressive heat of the living room. Everybody was standing, waiting desperately for the Benediction, which would signal the end of the formal part of the funeral. Sweat had now melted the starch in my shirt collar, swelling it into a warm, clammy paste that had a death grip on my neck.

My parents had arrived a few minutes before the minister, adding the oatmeal cookies to the growing mountain of food in the dining room. My mother had given me a suspicious once-over, trying to figure out why my clothes were still clean.

Much to everyone's relief, Reverend Karppinen finally ground out the Benediction. He fished out the handkerchief from his breast pocket again, wiped his forehead, and headed for the door, claiming that he had to give a eulogy at another funeral—probably just wanting to escape the heat in the Runkkinen house. As he was leaving, Lillian pressed a paper bag containing eighteen prune tarts into his hand.

The tension now eased considerably—neckties were loosened, coffee was poured, cigarettes and cigars were fired up, and people grabbed plates and picked over the massive array of sandwiches and baked goods in the dining room.

Several of the men found that they had urgent business in the Runkkinen woodshed, where, it was rumored, Jalmer kept a supply of homemade chokecherry wine.

Growing in great abundance around Ishpeming, chokecherries were about the size of a pea, with a large pit and not much fruit. They were tart enough to pucker a lemon, but in late summer when they ripened to a dark purple, Kippy and I would gorge ourselves on them, often resulting in first-class bellyaches. What they tasted like when fermented into wine, I couldn't even imagine.

But I soon found out what the smell was like. As guys came back from the woodshed from time to time, their breath enriched the lush assortment of aromas now permeating the house. I still hung around the coffin, but it was increasingly hard to tell if Elsie was going bad since several of the men *already* smelled like they were going bad .

My parents had some coffee and pastries but soon decided to leave since they weren't close friends of the Runkkinens. When I told my mother that I was going to hang around for awhile, her eyes narrowed into distrustful slits, but she couldn't fathom what I might be up to.

Lillian's disposition didn't perk up any as the afternoon wore on. Like all good Lutheran wives, she was dead set against drinking and wouldn't allow it in the house under any circumstances. Watching the men trooping through the kitchen on their way back and forth from the woodshed, faces flushed and eyes bloodshot, put her in an ugly mood, and while she would have relished bouncing a rolling pin off the heads of the more well-oiled kitchen tourists, she was too busy making fresh coffee, slicing rhubarb pie, and heating up prune tarts.

The weather deteriorated along with Lillian's temperament. Hostile, blue-black clouds loomed on the horizon, punctuated with flashes of lightning and grumbles of thunder in the distance.

Finally, Jalmer, who had been given marching orders by Lillian to stay sober under threat of severe bodily harm, walked into the living room and held up his hands.

"Folks, we're gonna hafta get the coffin up to the cemetery right away. If we wait too much longer, the rain's gonna hit, an' it'll be real tough t'close up the grave."

That pretty much broke up the funeral reception. Relatives and neighbors went up to the coffin, said one last goodbye to Elsie, gathered up their kids, and left. Violet went up and said one last goodbye to her good dress. The flowers were moved out of the way, and Jalmer and his brother Eli went out to the woodshed to get the coffin lid.

It was time for me to go home, but I just had to watch them put the lid on and ship Elsie off to the cemetery so I could give Kippy a complete funeral report. Besides, there was an almost-full cup of coffee that someone had left on the dining room table, and I was trying to figure out how to get a couple of swift gulps without anybody noticing.

Muzza and Blackie came back in with Jalmer and Eli since the four of them were to be the pall bearers. The curl on Lillian's upper lip hinted that Muzza and Blackie were not her top picks for the job since they had been out in the woodshed most of the afternoon taste-testing the chokecherry wine. They weren't even members of the immediate family, but Muzza drove a '36 Dodge pickup truck which was the closest thing anybody had that could be called into service as a hearse.

I didn't know about the truck, but both Muzza and Blackie were plenty gassed up for the trip to the cemetery: their eyes looked like road maps—both wore rubbery, slack-jawed grins—Muzza's Montgomery Ward suit was covered with sawdust from the woodshed floor—the tip of Blackie's necktie dangled from his shirt pocket where he had stuffed it.

Lillian grabbed the cup of coffee that I'd been eyeing and thrust it at Muzza. "Drink it! Elsie may be dead an' gone, but I want her to get out to the cemetery in one piece."

"Don' worry, missus. Elsie won't complain 'bout th'ride one bit—I guarantee." Muzza coughed out a raspy chuckle at his own wit until he locked eyes with Lillian. His grin dissolved, and he took a healthy swig of the coffee.

Jalmer and Eli screwed down the lid on the coffin, and the four of them grabbed the pall-bearer handles and carried it out into the enclosed front porch. They eased the front of the coffin out the door and down the five steps to the sidewalk just as a flash of lightning lit up the sky.

I spotted the tongue of the Radio Flyer wagon lying across the sidewalk, but Muzza, looking backward, didn't. As his right foot touched the sidewalk, it got tangled up with the wagon, and he lost his balance, which wasn't any too steady to begin with.

It still wouldn't have been too bad with three others carrying the coffin, but as Muzza was going down, he tried to stop the fall by hanging on to the pall-bearer handle. He gave the coffin a violent wrench which tore out the right front handle. This also pulled Jalmer's handle out of his grasp, and the front of the coffin hit the sidewalk with a splintery crash. Like a being on high commenting on the enormity of what had just happened, a horrendous clap of thunder followed.

Blackie and Eli quickly put the rear of the coffin down on the bottom step. Even from inside the porch I could see that the coffin was in bad shape. The right side had pulled loose from the front end-piece and had two ugly, wide splits in the wood. The coffin had sprung open like a packing crate that had fallen off the back end of a truck.

With the pall-bearer handle still in his left hand, Muzza looked down at the damage and clucked disapprovingly. "Now, don't that jus' go t'show ya? If Blackie had built it, a little bump like that wouldn't'a even put a dent in 'er—ain't that right, Blackie?"

Lillian looked up at the menacing sky, her lips moving, asking forgiveness for a sin that she was thinking about committing.

Clyde came up beside me and said in a loud whisper, "How d'ya think she's doin' in there? I betcha this is the first time that a dead body rolled over *before* it even got in tha grave."

Jalmer just stood there looking down at the coffin, with one hand cupping his cheek, shaking his head slowly. "My gawd! What're we gonna do?"

Blackie straightened up, walked to the front end of the coffin, and surveyed the damage. A transformation had come over him in the last minute. Gone was the bloodshot-eyed, slack-jawed drunk, and in his place was a businesslike, efficient craftsman with gritty determination.

Large raindrops smacked loudly on the coffin lid, but Blackie's voice rang out with authority over the gathering staccato drumming of the rain. "What're we gonna do, ya say? We're gonna *fix* it!"

Blackie immediately assumed the air of a chief surgeon about to perform a delicate operation. He fired instructions to the two sober pall bearers, Jalmer and Eli, on how to lift the devastated front end of the coffin while he and Muzza picked up the rear end off the porch step. They carefully guided it back up into the front porch.

"We're gonna bring 'er through all th'way into tha dining room an' put 'er on th'table," Blackie said.

"Wait a minute," Lillian snapped. "Can't you do this in...in the woodshed?"

"Not 'nough light in there. Dining room's got that ceiling lamp. Gotta see what I'm doin'...Olga, get that stuff off th'table."

Olga, Emily, and Violet quickly cleared off the dining room table, and the men set the coffin down on top. Blackie pulled the chain on the ceiling lamp and closely inspected the coffin.

"We gotta slide 'er over here, t'overhang th'edge of th'table so I can get a clamp on th'front end. Jalmer...I'm gonna need that big wood clamp you got in th'woodshed, th'rubber mallet, th'hand drill, th'set a bits, some inch-and-a-quarter wood screws..."

"But..." Lillian interrupted. "Aren't you...gonna...take Elsie out first?"

"No need disturbin' th'dead, missus," Blackie said, using an authoritarian tone designed to gain the confidence of everyone in the room...including Elsie. "I kin do this job, first class, without touchin' a hair on 'er head. Don' even haf'ta take th'lid off."

Jalmer lugged in the tools that Blackie had asked for, and the repairs on Elsie's coffin got underway. After some pushing and pounding with the rubber mallet, they got the split side board and the front end-piece lined up. The jaws of the big wood clamp went on the top and bottom of the coffin's front end and squeezed the whole thing back together. Obviously, Blackie knew his business because it looked pretty good. All that remained to be done was drill the screw holes in the side board, attach the side board to the end-piece with the wood screws, and then remount the pall-bearer handle.

Blackie, sensing that he was now in total control, decided to put his authority to the ultimate test. Flashing his most engaging grin, he said to Lillian, "Drillin' these holes is exactin' work, an' it's gonna take a steady hand. My hands'd be a lot steadier if I hadda glass a that chokecherry wine."

Lillian let loose with a defiant snarl. "Drinking in my house? I'll burn in hell first!"

Blackie locked her eyes with a take-charge stare. "You wanna get this job done today, er not?"

Jalmer interrupted. "I'll get the wine. Let's get this over with." He started for the back door.

"I believe I'll have a glass a that stuff, too," Muzza chimed in.

"Shaddup!" Lillian barked.

A minute later Jalmer came back with a quart milk bottle half full of chokecherry wine. Blackie took a jelly-jar glass from the cupboard, poured himself a healthy slug, and downed it in one gulp. Lillian stalked out into the front porch, and muttering to herself, arms folded across her chest, she stared out at the rain beating against the window panes.

Blackie drilled the holes for the wood screws, and had the job just about done when the chokecherry wine aroused his perfectionist nature.

"Jalmer, go get your countersink, a handful of sawdust, that white glue, and some varnish. We might as well do th'job right. I'll recess th'screw heads, mix up some wood paste, cover up th'screws, an' touch up th'spots with varnish. Ya won't even see where I put th'screws in—it'll be as smooth as a baby's butt."

Overhearing this, Lillian marched in from the porch. "Has it slipped your wine-soaked mind that this coffin's going six feet into the ground this afternoon? The reception's over—who cares what it looks like?"

"Ya never know who might see it on th'way t'tha cemetery."

Lillian jabbed a finger at Muzza. "It'll be in the back of his old pickup truck. The coffin *already* looks *twice* as good as the truck."

"Hey," Muzza said. "I jus' washed that truck yesterday."

Jalmer brought in the second batch of materials, and Blackie countersunk the holes, put in the screws, and covered them to his satisfaction. He picked up the can of varnish that Jalmer had brought in and wrinkled up his nose.

"Jalmer, this's maple varnish, an' th'coffin's walnut-colored. How's that gonna look?"

Lillian continued to mutter out in the porch.

Blackie and Muzza went out to the woodshed to look at the varnish supply, also taking the now-empty milk bottle along for a refill from the chokecherry wine crock.

Blackie found some varnish more to his liking and touched up the wood paste spots over the screw heads. The last thing that had to be done was to reattach the right front pall-bearer handle that Muzza had pulled off. Blackie looked at the handle and scratched his head thoughtfully, taking another gulp of wine.

"Y'know? The screws that Mattila used on these handles are too small. I think I'll take th'other three handles off and put 'em all back on with bolts. That way ya never hafta worry about 'em comin' loose again."

"Look," Jalmer said. "It's gonna be dark inna couple a hours. Can't ya just put that one handle back on?"

"Well...I guess so...but I'm still gonna bolt it on. We're gonna hafta take th'lid off so I kin thread a nut on th'end of th'bolt from the inside."

Take the lid off—that got everybody's attention. I had been wondering how well Elsie had survived the crash on the sidewalk, and so did everybody else, because a small crowd of people gathered around the dining room table as Blackie took the screws out of the lid.

He lifted off the lid. She looked about the same as when we last saw her about an hour ago...

Elsie's left hand raised up three inches.

Olga passed out right on the spot. Just slumped to the floor without a scream or anything. Then again, she never was much of a talker.

Muzza, holding the quart bottle of chokecherry wine, jumped straight back two feet from a flat-footed stance, slopping a good deal of the wine on the front of his Montgomery Ward suit.

Blackie blindly wheeled around to bolt into the kitchen, swinging the coffin lid that he was holding and narrowly missing Violet's head.

The four prune tarts and two pieces of rhubarb pie that I had eaten earlier clustered into a defensive knot in my stomach. Something warm trickled down my leg—I was glad I was wearing dark-blue pants.

Lillian stepped up and peered intently at Elsie. "Take it easy—take it easy—that's jus' a muscle spasm. I hear it happens sometimes when the bodies aren't embalmed. Probably 'cuz the coffin lid's been pressin' down on her hands. Don't worry, she's still dead." She pointed at Olga on the floor. "Jalmer, take her over to the sofa an' put some ammonia under her nose."

Blackie stood there, holding the coffin lid, looking uncertainly at Elsie. Lillian skewered him with a malicious smile. "Well, *Mister Master Carpenter*," she said sarcastically. "You're the one that wanted to fix every little thing on the coffin. Don't you wanna get in there an' put that handle on?"

Blackie nodded dumbly. He leaned the coffin lid against the wall and quickly went about drilling bolt holes for the handle, keeping one eye on Elsie all the time. When the handle was on, Blackie and Eli took the lid and placed it over the top of the coffin. But Elsie's left hand had now stiffened in its new position and kept the lid from seating properly on the coffin.

Blackie leaned over to Elsie's head and said in a soft, respectful lilt, "Put your hand down now, Aunt Elsie. It's time to go to th'cemetery."

After some gentle pushing, they got the coffin lid in place and quickly screwed it down. The rain had let up, and the four pall bearers quickly carried the coffin out to the pickup truck, loaded it, and drove off.

Lillian stood there at the front door for a moment as they disappeared down Second Street. She turned around and walked wearily into the kitchen, looking as if she had aged a lot that afternoon. Clyde was standing in the middle of the kitchen, holding the milk bottle half full of chokecherry wine, no doubt thinking about taking a slug.

"Gimme that!" Lillian hissed, snatching the bottle away from him. She slammed the bottle down on the kitchen table, looked at it for a second, and went over to the cupboard for a clean jelly-jar glass. Slumping down in a wooden chair, Lillian poured the glass full of wine and took a long, slow drink. She let out a sigh, massaged her temples, and stared vacantly at the pendulum of the Regulator clock on the kitchen wall.

The next day at Kippy's house, he and I were deep into our favorite afternoon snack, catsup sandwiches. Savoring mouthfuls of the spongy, white A&P bread, a luxury unavailable at my house since my mother baked all our bread, I gave him a complete rundown on the funeral.

"You kiddin' me? Her hand really came up—an' she was still dead?"

I nodded gravely, milking the narrative down to the last drop.

Kippy shook his head in unadulterated envy. "Boy! I wish I'd been there!"

Remembering what he'd said when he came back from his Aunt Beaulah's funeral and now being a crafty funeral veteran, I dismissed the topic with a casual wave of my hand. "It wasn't so much, though...if ya gotta strong stomach."

The Hill

*T*he Norwegian bent over and grabbed the edges of the starting-chute walls for maximum leverage on the push off. *"Bing-boing,"* the electronic tone signalled that the jumper was free to leave the chute, and with a frenzied push, the Norwegian launched himself onto the steep main track, pumping his skis a few times to get up speed. He shot down the track of the ninety-meter scaffold, his body coiled low to the skis. Hitting the takeoff point, his thighs exploded with power, sending his upper torso out over the skis, arms straight back next to his body. His golden, skin-tight suit had a silver headpiece, and as he soared through the air at tree-top level, he looked like a gliding bald eagle, searching for prey.

CBS switched cameras, giving the television viewers a shot from below. Then I saw it. The backs of the Norwegian's skis were almost touching in flight, but the tips were about six feet apart, forming a ragged-looking V.

The coffee cup stopped halfway to my mouth. My gawd—he's lost control—his skis aren't even *close* to being parallel! He'll be lucky to pull out of this one!

But the Norwegian didn't even try to recover. He kept the skis in the V, only straightening them out just before the landing. He touched down in classical Scandinavian telemark style—the crowd cheering and whistling.

A CBS announcer, dressed in a plum-colored, padded jacket with matching woolen cap, smiled into the camera:

Good afternoon, ladies and gentlemen, and welcome to the opening round of the ninety-meter ski jumping event here at Courchevel, France, at the 1992 Winter Olympics. You have just seen the first jumper using the new V-configuration technique which, they say, improves the jumper's aerodynamic lift, extending the distance...

For crissake—he did that on *purpose*? When I was jumping, my skis used to look like that V—among other unplanned odd angles that I put them in. The other kids laughed like hell at each new innovative formation I used in midair because they always relished the disastrous landings. Was I simply fifty years ahead of my time? I perched on the edge of the couch with interest.

The next jumper shot out over the steep landing area, body straining forward to gain every extra meter he could muster. Instinctively, my body fell into concert with the jumper, straining forward out over the coffee table, feeling the stiff, icy wind in my face flicking back the pages on the calendar...

A brain-numbing north wind howled down Second Street. I swiped at my runny nose with the sleeve of my snowsuit and pulled the woolen muffler back up over my face. By now the mouth moisture on the inside of the scarf had frozen, and I sucked on wool-flavored ice pellets as I energetically packed down the snow on the top of the takeoff point, or bump as we called it, with the back of my new, short-handled snow shovel.

The shovel was a Christmas present from the old man. He had earlier explained that every grown man had to have a snow shovel of his very own, and therefore I was delighted when I saw it under the tree last month. For two weeks I used it to furiously attack the snow on the path between the kitchen door and the street, until one day it dawned on my six-and-a-half-year-old brain that I was now doing the job that the old man had been stuck with before Christmas. I was obviously no match for his resourceful, devious nature.

But now the shovel was being put to better use in the construction of an architectural masterpiece. My pal, Kippy Jacobs, and I were applying the finishing touches on our first ski jump, on the sloping snow-covered embankment of the Lake Superior & Ishpeming Railroad tracks that ran between our houses at the end of Second Street in Ishpeming. Using snow, I had painstakingly constructed the bump, resembling a miniature cliff halfway down the embankment, while Kippy stood at the top, carving steps into the side of a two-foot-high scaffold, also made out of blocks of snow. It made a precipitous eight-foot drop, but we were Upper Michigan men—born and bred to scoff at danger.

Kippy jammed the blade of his shovel into the snow. "C'mon—tha's good nuff—it's gettin' dark, an' we ain't even tried it yet."

"OK. We gonna flip a penny t'see who goes first?"

"You gotta penny?"

"Yup," but my penny was in a leather coin purse in the pocket of my shirt, buried beneath seventeen layers of sweaters under the woolen snow-suit. I yanked off my mittens with my teeth, letting them hang by the strings that my mother had sewn on—I hated those strings, but she'd promised me that next winter she'd take them off. Pulling down the front zipper of the snowsuit, I tried to burrow my hand underneath the layers of sweaters to get at the shirt pocket. But my arm, encased in all that wool, wouldn't bend enough, so Kippy attacked the problem from the front, sticking his hand up beneath my sweaters to get the coin purse.

Our kitchen door popped open, and my mother stuck her head out. "What in the world are you kids doing out there? Zip up that snowsuit right now! You'll catch your death of pneumonia!"

Even after being threatened with it countless times, I still had no idea what pneumonia was, but we quickly got the penny out and I zipped up the snowsuit. Putting the penny on my thumbnail, I looked at Kippy, pre-pared for the solemn, momentous occasion.

"I want heads," Kippy said.

I flipped the penny into the air, and it landed on the hard-packed snow.

"Hah!" Kippy barked triumphantly. "Heads—I win! *You* go first!"

I waddled over to my skis, stuck upright in a snowbank at the foot of the jump. My very first ski jump—I was on the brink of manhood! I critically inspected the scarred and chipped maple skis that the old man had picked up in a clever trade for a bushel of potatoes. He and I had scored a two-to-one victory over my mother in the debate over the wisdom of ski jumping, in general, and the advisability of me taking it up, in particular.

"You'll kill yourself!" she'd shrilled.

"All tha kids're doin' it!" I'd cleverly countered.

The old man finally broke the deadlock of wills by pointing out that if I was going to kill myself ski jumping, I might as well do it now, while the two of them were still young enough to have another kid.

Steeling myself for the trial, I grabbed the skis and bravely trudged up the embankment. Originally, the skis were seven feet long, but since I was only knee-high to a fire plug, the old man had sawed a foot and a half off the back ends, giving the skis suspenseful balance characteristics now that the foot placements were at the rear.

I laid the skis on the snow scaffold, tips pointing down the hill, and climbed up onto the scaffold, putting my galoshes into the toe straps. These skis weren't exactly designed for jumping, with no foot binders whatsoever but only cracked leather toe straps.

Inching the tips of the skis over the edge, I looked down at Kippy for moral support.

"C'mon, ya chicken, it's gettin' dark," he yelled.

I clamped my teeth down on my muffler to keep it from flapping in the wind, and surged forward.

It lasted no more than three seconds, but it felt like three days. Apparently, we had put too much upturn on the bump, and that, combined with the fact that I was falling backward when I reached it, shot me straight up into the air, where I executed a nifty end-over-end flip, making a perfect one-point landing in the snow—on my head. The skis flew off into the twilight.

Agonizingly, I rolled over onto my elbows, digging a pound of snow out of my right ear. "How far'd I go?" I croaked.

Kippy pulled out a wooden ruler and studiously measured off the distance. "Well...yer head hit the snow about..."—he moved the ruler two times—"two and a half feet from the bump."

"Two and a half feet? On the very first try? Hey! Tha's pretty good!"

On Friday night the old man and I sat at the kitchen table while my mother fried hash on the cast-iron wood stove. I particularly liked Friday suppers because my mother was finally forced to capitulate on the roast beef hash in its usual warmed-over status and fry it in patties. The old man religiously bought a beef roast every week for Sunday's dinner, and just as religiously, my mother ground up the leftovers into hash every Monday morning. Monday's, Tuesday's, and Wednesday's warmed-up hash wasn't too bad, but by Thursday, rigor mortis had set in, stiffening it badly, requiring a lot of catsup to get it down. But Friday's fried hash was a whole new delicacy. I was a connoisseur of fried hash.

My mother put the plates on the table, and the old man experimentally probed the crust of a hash patty with his fork. "So, how far are ya jumpin'?"

I beamed proudly. "This afternoon I got over five feet!"

His fork stopped in midair. "Five feet, eh? Tha's pretty good! Izzat where the backs a the skis hit the snow?"

"Uh...no...that's where my bum hits the snow."

He plunged the fork into the hash patty and began to saw off a piece with his knife. "Ya don't measure a jump to where yer *backside* hits the snow. Ya measure it to where the ends a the *skis* hit the snow."

I got excited. "Oh, yeah? Wow! Then the jumps're much longer cause the skis really go flyin'!"

"Whaddaya mean? Don't they stay on yer feet?"

"Uh...no...they go flyin' off...every time."

"I *told* you he's gonna kill himself!" my mother yelled.

"Yah—this'll do the trick!" The old man reached into the mountainous rat's nest of "good stuff" that he had collected in a corner of the woodshed over the years and pulled out a liberally patched inner tube.

It was the following afternoon, and my mother had delivered the ultimatum that either he had to figure out a way to keep the skis from flying off of my feet, or my ski-jumping days were over. Kippy had the same problem with his skis, and so we both watched with intense interest as the old man laid the inner tube on the work bench, took out his jackknife, and started carving it up into inch-wide rubber bands.

When he had cut out four bands, two for me and two for Kippy, he put one of my skis on the woodshed floor and placed a band so that it lay on top of the ski, encircling the outside of the toe strap.

"Put yer boot into the strap."

I inserted the toe of one of my galoshes into the strap, stepping down on the inner tube rubber band, which was now trapped between the sole of the boot and the leather toe strap. The old man then lifted my boot heel, stretched the inner tube band back, snapped the back of the band over the heel of my boot and adjusted it up about three inches from the bottom of the sole.

Experimentally, I lifted my leg, and the ski, now bound to my foot with the rubber binder, came up with it.

"Hey, that's neat! Will the skis stay on when I go over the bump?"

The old man bared his upper plate in a modest grin. "Bet'cher life!"

Kippy and I grabbed our skis and the old man's innovative rubber binders and ran out to the ski jump. If the skis stayed on our feet, who knew what might happen—we might even be able to complete the jump without falling on our rear ends.

I scrambled to the top of the snow scaffold, put on the skis, and snapped the rubber binders over the heels of my galoshes. Without a moment's hesitation, I launched myself down the slope, confident that this was going to be a record-setting jump.

A split second after I shot out over the bump, the major drawback of using rubber binders became crystal clear. While they kept the skis on my feet, they had little effect on keeping the skis from rotating laterally once I was airborne. In fact, the ski tips perversely crossed just before I landed.

Now, anyone who knows anything at all about ski jumping will tell you that you lose a lot of style points if your ski tips are crossed. Not only that, but you tend to decelerate very quickly. This has a bad effect on your balance, and your general state of health, for that matter.

I hit the landing, and the crossed ski tips ground to a complete stop. Since my feet were now connected to the toe straps with the rubber binders, the laws of physics caused my body to spring forward like the business end of a mousetrap—my upper two front teeth making a respectable attempt at removing a mouthful of maple from the front end of one of the skis.

A cloud of snow slowly settled over my body as I lay there, listening to my teeth scream. Kippy came over with the wooden ruler. "I don' know how t'measure that one. Ya look like ya hit everyplace at once."

Kippy and I worked at jumping all day Saturday. But the rubber binders turned the skis into little devils, and if the ski tips didn't cross on the jump, the backs of the skis did. I spent most of the day plowing furrows in the snow with my nose.

Clouds of steam drifted up from the washtub half full of hot water, sitting on the kitchen floor next to the stove. It was the dreaded Saturday-night bath, and as soon as I came in from the ski jump, my mother started peeling off my layers of clothes. She paused and looked closely at my face.

"You been fighting with those Catholic kids again?"

"Nope."

"Then why is your lip all bloody?"

"Ski jumpin'. Sometimes m'face gets mashed into the front a the skis."

She pulled on my lower lip and looked inside. "Omigawd! Your front teeth have chewed up the inside of your lip! You know, those are your second set of teeth, and if you lose those, you don't get any more."

That was bad news. I always figured that teeth kept growing back as you lost them.

She took off my wool shirt and stared at the curious wet bulge on the front of my long underwear. "What's that?"

"Uh...snow."

"Why in the world did you stuff snow inside your underwear?"

"Didn't put it there—it got there from the ski jumping."

She unbuttoned the front of the underwear and scooped out the snow. "I don't know much about ski jumping, but I'll bet that most ski jumpers don't go around with snow packed in their underwear."

"It gets there when I slide on my face on the landing."

"I thought your pa fixed those skis so you wouldn't be falling down all the time."

"Well...the rubber binders keep the skis on my feet, but they still wiggle-waggle from side to side."

"These binders...are they usually made out of rubber?"

"Uh...no...if ya buy 'em, they're iron or sumthin'. Pop made mine outta an old inner tube in the woodshed."

Slowly, she got up and stalked over to the old man who was sitting at the kitchen table, studiously rolling a cigarette and trying to be as invisible as possible.

"Wha...how'ja get those?" Kippy salivated as he looked down at the metal binders on my skis.

"Pop got 'em yesterday."

"Boy, he must'a been feelin' pretty good."

"No...I don' think he wuz feelin' very good at all, but ma tol' 'im to buy the binders...or else." I lifted up one leg and shook my foot and the ski around. The ski moved like it was part of my body now. I skied quickly through the yard over to the ski jump. This was it! I had all of the right equipment now—I was going to become a real ski jumper!

It worked. On the third try I kept my balance and stayed upright through the whole ride. With true Lutheran style and grace, I nonchalantly glanced over at Kippy as if it were just another jump, but my heart was trying to leap out through the seventeen layers of wool.

With only one pair of metal binders, Kippy and I had to take turns using my skis, but that was all right. The new binders kept the skis pointed steady, and from then on, almost every jump was a new record. Our mothers practically had to drag us into the house for supper, long after it had gotten dark.

Ski jumping in the dark is not a sport for the faint of heart. Since you can't see the landing, you have to stay in the crouch after you leave the takeoff point, prepared for the snow to suddenly reach up and smack you at any moment. You could always spot a kid who practiced ski jumping in the dark—he would walk around hunched over like Groucho Marx, looking cautiously at the ground at every step, only resuming an erect posture around Memorial Day.

Finally, one afternoon in late January, Kippy stated what was becoming obvious to us both.

"We're not gonna be able t'get any bigger jumps on this hill—it's too small."

I knew he was right, but my mind wouldn't accept it. "Let's build the scaffold bigger."

"We build it any bigger, it'll cover one a the rails, an' the ore trains'll smash it down."

"But...I'm jumpin' eight feet now...I *gotta* get ten feet 'fore the winter's over."

"Guess we gotta find a bigger hill, then," Kippy said.

In unspoken unison, we both turned and looked to the south. There, looming against the purple twilight of the low winter sun, it stood—*The Hill.*

The Hill was a ski jump built on a bluff south of the LS&I tracks. Its towering size and steepness gave it an ugly, brooding appearance, dwarfing our puny little jump on the track embankment. All the kids who jumped on The Hill were several years older than Kippy and I and had already demonstrated a natural talent for the sport. Even so, The Hill would occasionally lash out and snap a leg bone of a cocky young jumper who had started to take it for granted. This aroused the blood lust in the nearby residents, and when the kids were jumping, there were always a handful of onlookers waiting for The Hill to exact its toll.

With Ishpeming, Michigan, being one of the prominent ski-jumping centers in the country, the question was never *whether* a kid would take up jumping—it was *at what age.* Men gathered around in Salo's Barber Shop had conversations like:

"How old's yer boy now, Matt?"

"Jus' turned four in December."

"Four, eh? He must'a started jumpin' this winter."

"Well...no...the wife sez she wants 'im t'getta li'l more practice walkin' yet."

"Too bad...them women, eh? Next winter fer sure though."

"You bet!"

So you can see that at six and a half, I was considered a late bloomer.

Conversely, unless a kid was one of the few truly gifted jumpers, the day would arrive when he would stare at a ski jump that scared the pee out of him and quietly opt for retirement from the sport.

Such was the case with The Hill. Many a brash, young squirt who had sneeringly mastered a small neighborhood ski jump similar to the one Kippy and I had built, took one look at The Hill, meekly turned the skis over to a younger brother, and took up a more sedate sport like hockey.

Kippy broke the silence. "Ya must'a landed on yer head too many times if yer thinkin' 'bout ridin' The Hill."

I kept staring, trancelike, at The Hill. "Dunno—I ain't fell down on this one in 'bout a week."

"In case ya ain't noticed, The Hill makes this one look like a mosquito bite lump. It's fer the big kids."

"I could get ten feet easy on it."

"Ya'd be ten feet *under* the snow after ya hit the landing. 'Sides, Tommy ain't gonna let ya on The Hill even if yer crazy 'nough t'try it."

He had a point there. Tommy La Brut, the ten-year-old head thug of the South Ishpeming French and Italian gang, was the self-declared landlord of The Hill. The unwritten rules were that unless you were Catholic or considerably bigger than Tommy, you didn't ride The Hill. I didn't qualify in either category.

"Let's ask 'im anyway."

Kippy took off the skis and handed them to me. "*You* ask 'im. I'll watch from my kitchen window."

Cheeko Bussiere stood at the top of The Hill and slid his skis back and forth to kick the snow out of the bottom grooves. A gust of wind out of the north swirled his hair around. It was a refreshing five degrees below zero, but none of the kids who rode The Hill wore caps, since it would be considered a sign of weakness. Cheeko shoved off and shot down The Hill. When he reached the bump, his body straightened out, and he windmilled his arms furiously as he flew out over the landing. He landed perfectly and skied to a stop.

This was the following afternoon after school, and I had quietly sidled up to Tommy La Brut, who was leaning on a snow shovel next to The Hill's bump.

"How far'd he go?" I asked timidly.

Tommy spat a dark-brown gob into the snow, demonstrating that he was now old enough to take up chewing tobacco. "A piss-poor jump...'bout twenty feet." Then it dawned on him that he had just responded to a question from a first-grader, which he categorized as a lower life form. He puckered his eyes into his usual, mean George Raft squint and stared down at me. "Whaddaya doin' up here, snot nose?"

I didn't hear the question. *Twenty feet! If Cheeko could do twenty feet on a bad jump, I could jump ten feet easy. I had to ride The Hill!*

"I'm talkin' t'ya, small fry." Tommy attempted to give me a vicious finger jab to the chest, but only succeeded in burying a forefinger deep into the many layers of sweaters.

I crossed my fingers inside my mitten. "Kin I take a ride? I got iron binders now."

"Kin ya take a ride?" Tommy summoned up an extra load of saliva and nailed one of my galoshes with a stream of tobacco juice. "Fat chance!" If ya tried t'ride The Hill, ya'd poop yer pants, an' we'd haf'ta clean it off th'landing."

I raised myself up to my full three-foot-eleven-inch height. "I ain't afraid a The Hill."

Tommy reached down and picked up what looked like a snowball, except the sunlight glinting off the surface gave it a more businesslike appearance. "Ya know what this is?"

I nodded. Everybody in the neighborhood recognized an ore-ball—a lethal invention of the local French-Italian gang. An ore-ball was made by molding a snowball around a chunk of iron ore—plentiful around the railroad tracks. Water was then poured on the ball to form a thick, hard shell of ice, creating a high-density, aerodynamically perfect missile of destruction. Removing the wooden siding of Protestant houses with ore-balls was Tommy's favorite winter pastime.

Hovering over me, Tommy ominously hefted the ore-ball in his right hand. "If ya don' high-tail it fer home right now, I'm gonna let ya have this right in th'kisser."

Quickly, I scuttled away. Getting an ore-ball in the kisser was a serious matter, although I had my doubts that he would have thrown one at me. Making an ore-ball properly was a time-consuming, exacting craft, and no one wasted them on frivolous targets such as first-graders.

Tommy fired a parting shot. "I CATCH YA TRYIN' T'RIDE THE HILL, I'LL KICK YER ASS FROM HERE T'NEGAUNEE!"

The thrill was gone from our jump on the track embankment. I had definitely mastered it, but an eight-foot leap was all the little ski jump had in it. The Hill whispered to me enticingly. *Ten feet easy...maybe fifteen ...maybe twenty...*

The solution was elegant in its simplicity. Tommy's oldest sister was getting married on the first Saturday in February, and Tommy would undoubtedly be at the church that afternoon for the wedding. I'd sneak a ride on The Hill when Tommy was at church, get the ten-foot jump under my belt, and no one would be the wiser. I chuckled at my ingenuity—what could possibly go wrong with such a perfect plan?

The fateful Saturday rolled around, and by four o'clock in the afternoon the coast was clear. Kippy and I grabbed the skis with the metal binders and hurriedly sneaked up to The Hill. We didn't have any time to waste since the sun was already getting low—The Hill was not one to tolerate someone jumping it in bad light.

Kippy, being the older and wiser, figured that the smart thing to do was to see if I survived before he took the gamble, so I shouldered the skis and trudged up to the top. I hurriedly buckled up the binders and skied over to the edge of the upper track. Only then did I get my first good look from the business end of The Hill.

The Hill

I was standing on top of a forty-story skyscraper, ski tips jutting out over the edge, about to ski down the side of the building. Somewhere, deep down in my gut, last night's fried hash did a slow roll and decided to start crawling back up the way it came in. My right leg twitched uncontrollably, and even though the usual, icy north wind was blowing into my face, I started to sweat. Frantically, I looked down at Kippy, hoping that he'd beg me not to try it, but no, he was just standing patiently at the bottom, waiting for what would undoubtedly be my last jump. I didn't know how I was going to get out of it, but one thing I knew for sure—there was no way I was going to ride down The Hill on skis.

"I TOL' YA I'D POUND YA IF YA CAME UP HERE AGAIN! GET OFFA THAT HILL!" Tommy La Brut stepped off the railroad tracks beyond the landing of The Hill and marched purposefully toward me. Kippy was nowhere to be seen.

Why wasn't Tommy in church? I wished *I* was in church. Wait a second—Tommy's early arrival was a blessing in disguise! His pounding couldn't possibly be any worse than trying to ski down The Hill.

With a sigh of relief I began to back away from the edge of The Hill, but it must have been a combination of not having much practice backing up on skis and the sudden swirl of wind from behind, because both of my skis lost traction and shot forward. I fell down on the backs of the skis, and for one brief moment, teetered on the edge before plunging down the upper track.

As I rocketed down The Hill toward the bump, sitting on the backs of the skis, I quickly assessed the situation, opened my mouth, and uttered...

EEEEIIIIAAAAAAAHHHHHHH!!!!!

My whole life passed before my eyes—taking only a fraction of a second since I hadn't done all that much in six and a half years. I scrunched my eyes shut and braced for sudden death.

I shot over the bump—a screaming, large, woolly cannonball with madly gyrating appendages of maple skis and mittens on strings. I had so much backspin that when I first hit the landing I bounced off to the right, churning up snow, disintegrating several sticker bushes, and pulverizing old man Heikkinen's mail box. Fifteen pounds of snow jammed up my nose and into my mouth.

29

I was standing on top of a forty-story skyscraper, ski tips jutting out over the edge.

Finally, it felt as if I had stopped, but it couldn't be since something was still pummelling my rib cage. I opened my eyes—I *had* stopped—Tommy La Brut was leaning over me, delivering rapid-fire body punches. Seeing that the punches weren't penetrating my immense layer of wool padding, he cocked a fist and was taking aim at my nose when Kippy came up behind him and whacked him across the butt with the blade of a snow shovel. Tommy jumped up and took off after Kippy, a futile effort, because when it came to outdistancing bullies, Kippy was an established Olympic-class sprinter.

My head cleared, and it slowly dawned on me what had just happened. A smile inched across my face as I lay in the snow, blood dripping from my nose, with half a splintered ski dangling from my right foot.

I had ridden The Hill and survived!

Ninety-six meters by Matti Nukkenen, a fantastic young jumper from Finland—only sixteen years old! The crowd is giving a big hand to this courageous young man...

The CBS announcer broke the trance, and I found myself still leaning over the coffee table. I settled back on the couch, sipped the cold coffee, and watched them heap adulation on the young skier from Finland.

Well, Matti, you look good alright...*have* to be to get into the Olympics. I didn't quite reach the ninety-meter class myself, but then again, I had *retired* from ski jumping long before I was sixteen.

I don't know about that courageous part, though, Matti. I wonder how you'd feel about trying that hill with nothing but toe straps on the skis—or how about rubber binders? Or in the dark? For sheer excitement, Matti, you've got to try ski jumping in the dark sometime.

Would you have enough moxie to go down the hill if some eight-foot Frenchman was standing at the bottom, waiting to beat the crap out of you when you landed?

I dunno, Matti...I suppose this would all sound like sour grapes to you, and maybe I'm just an old curmudgeon, but I'm afraid you were born too late. They've taken all the grit out of the sport.

Monday Millionaires and the Case of the Mysterious Meatball

*I*jes' seen yer hubby come outta the Hematite Heaven Bar...the sidewalk wuz real slick from the rain, an' he didn't look none too steady."

Bertha wet her lips to let us know that she was getting to the juicy part. "Well, he slipped an' would'a took an awful spill, 'cept he grabbed a lamppost—then he couldn't let go. He jes kept hangin' onto the lamppost like he wuz afraid a fallin' off the world."

When it came to stirring up trouble in Ishpeming, Michigan, nobody had a bigger spoon than Bertha Maki. Normally, her specialty was news releases on unmarried mothers and shotgun weddings, but when the romance business was slow, she branched out into bankruptcies, bar fights, and benders like the one my old man was on. We hadn't seen him since yesterday, and Bertha had just confirmed our suspicions with her latest sighting. The old man only drank about once a year when, without warning, he'd receive a whispered summons from some Finnish Bacchus and go on a bender for two or three days.

The old man conducted his benders in the traditional Finnish style, requiring that you take a leave of absence from family, job, and social obligations to devote yourself entirely to some serious drinking. A successful bender depended on three critical factors.

First, you never announced your bender beforehand, like approaching your wife and saying, "Honeybunch, I won't be around for the next five or six days because I'm going on a bender." The chances are there wouldn't be any bender at all because the only thing that would get bent would be the frying pan your honeybunch used on the side of your head.

Second, benders always should be conducted in secret locations, so as not to be interrupted by wives or bosses—deer-hunting camps are good.

Finally, you never returned from a bender too early while your wife was still in an unreasonable state of mind and hadn't had a chance to start worrying. Coming back too early could result in severe physical injury or even death.

My mother took in the firsthand account while she poured Bertha a cup of coffee. After a minute, she started grinding her upper and lower dentures together, an ominous sound like a cartridge being levered into a rifle chamber. This was not a good sign. I got up and edged toward the living room. Somebody could get hurt when she did that, and I didn't want it to be me.

She slammed the fire-blackened coffee pot back on the wood stove, stomped over to the cupboard, jerked open the glass-paned door, and pulled out *the sugar bowl.*

This sugar bowl was the family bank, where my mother and the old man made deposits and withdrawals for major investments like clothes and furniture. She dumped out the bills and coins on the oilcloth-covered kitchen table and did a quick count. "Seven dollars...he took seven dollars...*he took seven dollars!*"

This was 1941—embezzling seven dollars from the sugar bowl was not petty thievery; it was grand larceny. She left the money on the table and just stood staring out the window, bouncing up and down on the balls of her feet like an idling car engine in need of a tune up. Her eyes drifted to the hook on the back of the kitchen door. Coiled around the hook was the old man's truss.

"Look at that—he didn't even have enough sense to wear his truss!"

Years ago, the old man had gotten a hernia working out in the logging camps and to keep his innards from pooching out, had a truss—a curious-looking device, composed of a heavy, leather-covered metal weight attached to the end of a belt of spring steel. The weight pressed into the rupture and was kept in place by the tension of the springy steel belt.

My mother snatched it off the hook, took hold of one end of the belt, and shook it out like a bull whip. The metal weight on the other end of the spring steel danced a couple of inches off the floor.

"Seven dollars...and he's just drinking it away. He's got a ruptured *brain* is what he's got, and the next time I see him, that's where I'm gonna stick this truss!" With a lightning-quick overhand motion, she swung the truss over her head, and the weight on the other end whistled through the air.

KAPOOOOWWWWWWW!!!!!!!!!

The weight hit the top of the stove like an enormous rifle slug. Three stove lids, the coffee pot, and Bertha Maki jumped into the air. Bertha finished her coffee with one gulp and squeaked, "Well, thanks a lot fer th'coffee. I guess I'd better run along."

I also ran along—for cover—up to my bedroom.

An hour later when I figured it was safe, I crept back downstairs. My mother was dividing the sugar bowl money into piles on the kitchen table. She handed me the movie theater advertisement for Marquette County that we got every week in the mail. "Did you see this?"

"Yeah." I always studied the Saturday matinee billing at the Ishpeming Theater. It was vitally important to know which cowboy heroes were being featured.

"Would you like to see that new Jack Benny movie?"

"*Charlie's Aunt*? You bet! But it's in Negaunee, not here. It's at night. You don' lemme go to the movies at night."

"It's summer; you can stay up a little later this once."

"But Ma, it's in Negaunee. We gonna walk there?"

She put one of the piles of coins and bills in her purse and the rest back in the sugar bowl. "Your pa likes to spend money. Well, two can play that game. Tomorrow night we're gonna take the Four Hundred to Negaunee."

Kippy Jacobs' mouth hung open while he tried to grasp the sheer enormity of what I had just told him. "Ya mean yer gonna *ride* on the Four Hundred?"

"Yup—t'Negaunee tomorrow night." This was the most incredible event that had happened to me in my whole life, and I had run over to Kippy's house to tell him the news.

The Four Hundred was the newly operational diesel streamliner, running from Ishpeming to Chicago and named for the four-hundred-mile trip. I had been on it once, months ago, when they had an open house before the maiden run. The train sat at the Ishpeming depot while the total population of Marquette County trooped through it. Iron miners trod reverently down the plush-carpeted aisles, stroking the luxurious gray-velvet seats with the snowy-white doilies draped over the backs to blot up excess hair tonic. In the dining car, black waiters stood ramrod stiff in starched, white uniforms. Black people were such an utter rarity in the Upper Peninsula in those days that some folks made the trip to the depot just to see the dining car staff.

"But Negaunee's only three miles from here," Kippy said. "How come yer ma's gonna buy train tickets 'stead a jus' walkin' there?"

"She's mad at pop fer takin' seven dollars outta the sugar bowl fer his bender. She sez that, startin' tomorrow, *we're* gonna spend money like drunks, too. Ain't that great?"

Kippy whistled. "Seven dollars! Whaa... He mus' figure on bein' gone a long time. Ya think he's comin' back?"

"I think so...but ya know what else we're gonna do?" My whole body was vibrating with anticipation.

"What?"

"We're gonna have supper over at the Mather Inn before we get on the Four Hundred."

If you wanted to eat high on the hog in Marquette County, there was no better place than the Mather Inn in Ishpeming. A huge, colonial-style red-brick building with towering white columns flanking the front entrance, it had strategically placed dining-room windows to give the working class a glimpse of those who could afford to eat there. Everybody in the dining room dressed like they had just come from a wedding or a funeral.

This was too much for Kippy to absorb at one time. "Eat at the Mather Inn? On'y millionaires eat there. Yer lyin'!"

"Am not! If ya don' believe me, come down at six o'clock an' you can see us through the window. I'll wave to ya."

That got him. "Hey, kin ya bring me some leftovers?"

"Sure. I'm gonna save somethin' for th'dog, too."

I tore my eyes off the railroad tracks and shot a glance over at the sleek, camouflage-colored ME 109 German fighter plane hedgehopping alongside about one hundred yards to my right. I was at the controls in the locomotive of the Four Hundred, racing the fighter across Upper Michigan countryside to some unknown destination.

The fighter bounced up and down as the German maneuvered over barns and farmhouses at three hundred miles an hour. He was good, I had to admit, but he was no match for me at the throttle of the Four Hundred. I inched the throttle forward and the streamliner started to pull ahead of the low-flying airplane.

The German pilot pulled back the cockpit canopy, the wind pummelling the white scarf he had around his neck. He turned his head toward me and in perfect English, yelled...

"TIME FOR BREAKFAST!"

I opened my eyes and stared at the peeling wallpaper that the old man had put up in my bedroom last year. Then I remembered...today was Monday, the day my mother and I were going to go out and spend money like drunks, climaxed with a ride on the Four Hundred to Negaunee to see Jack Benny.

My mother yelled again. "GET UP! BREAKFAST'S ON THE TABLE."

I jumped out of bed and into my clothes, eagerly anticipating the day's excesses. As I dashed for the stairs, I was struck with a chilling thought. What if the old man had come home last night after I went to bed? What if she had already clobbered him with the truss and the big spending plans are all off?

I tiptoed into their bedroom—the bed was already made. Good...the old man must still be gone, because if he had come back, he'd still be in bed. Benders made him very tired.

My mother was in the kitchen ironing her best slip. This was a sure sign that some serious gallavanting was on the horizon. "Sit down and eat your cereal. We've got a lot to do today."

"Why don't I run down to the Busy Bee an' get us some hamburgers fer breakfast?"

"Eat your cereal."

"Aren't we gonna spend money today?"

"Yes, but not on hamburgers. We're gonna start by buying you something else."

"Oh, yeah? Whaddar we gonna get me? A model airplane?"

"Not exactly."

The clerk in the boy's clothing department gave my mother a buttery smile. "We've got some nice gabardine suits, just in...."

She cut him off. "Don't want gabardine. Bring out something in heavy wool. After today, the next time he'll be wearing a suit will be Christmas, and it'll be ten below zero."

"But Ma," I whimpered, "it's July..."

"One night in a wool suit's not gonna kill you."

Minutes later, the clerk came out with a brown, double-breasted suit. He held the coat, and I slipped into it.

Flashing a self-satisfied grin, the clerk oozed, "Ah...fits perfectly. I can usually size them up pretty good as soon as they come in..."

"It's too small," she said.

The grin faded. "Well...it looks very good to me..."

"You got any kids?" she snapped.

"Ah...no..."

"Well, then there's something you ought'a know about kids. They *grow*. By Christmas, his wrists'll be sticking outta the sleeves of this coat, and since we're not made outta money like his father seems to think we are, the suit'll have to last awhile. Bring out something bigger."

She decided on a dark-blue suit—my fingertips reached the elbow of the inside of the coat sleeves. The pants were so big that I could look down inside the waistband and see my bare legs.

The material was a half-inch thick. At least two hundred sheep had sacrificed their wool to make that suit. Now I knew why sheepmen always moved in on the cattle ranges during the Saturday matinees. They had to expand their spread just to raise enough wool for my mother.

"Get those cuffs on right away. We'll be back this afternoon to pick it up," she told the clerk as she paid for the suit.

"Where to now?" I asked, hoping that the spending spree was going to take a more savory turn.

"To the sauna."

"I'm dyin'...I can't breathe!"

My mother jabbed the tip of a soapy washcloth in my ear and reamed it out. "Shut up and stand still."

If anybody in Ishpeming wanted to know firsthand what hell was like, they only had to rent a room in the public sauna on First Street. The temperature was nine hundred degrees in the steam-filled room, and I was sweating a gallon a minute, shrinking like an ice cube. If my mother thought that the new suit was on the large side when we bought it, wait till she saw me in it now. I'd fit in one of the sleeves.

The sauna cost a quarter, so it was a luxury we didn't indulge in very often. I was still washtub size, which was how I got my bath every Saturday night, in the middle of the kitchen floor. Only when I got dirty enough to warrant a steam cleaning did my mother bring me down to the sauna.

"Ain't we done yet?" I whined.

"You're a Finn. You're supposed to like saunas."

"I *hate* saunas. Maybe I ain't a Finn."

She ignored that and waved her hand toward the stairs that led up to a small, raised platform in the back of the room. "When you're older, you'll want to go up there."

"Why?"

"It's hotter."

"Hotter than right here? I ain't *never* gonna get that old! Boy, I bet when the Finns catch spies, they bring 'em in the sauna an' put 'em up there t'make 'em talk."

"I dunno about that, but when I catch your father, I think I'll put him up there and make *him* talk. OK, I'll rinse you off." She took a pail of water and dumped it over my head.

In my parboiled state, the water felt as cold as liquid nitrogen. My heart stopped in mid beat. I opened my mouth to scream, but my vocal chords were paralyzed.

My mother busily towelled my sopping-wet head. "Hmmm...your hair's getting pretty long..."

My body went totally rigid as the barber pumped the large lever on the side of the chrome and leather chair, inching it upward so he could better lay his hands on my defenseless head. This was just like the dentist!

Sensing my terror, he said, "Take it easy, young fella. With these new electric clippers I got, it'll be all over before y'know it."

Be all over? What did he mean by that? I looked down at the floor which was getting further away by the second. Should I jump and make a run for it?

The barber proudly held up the clippers—a very large silver beetle without eyes but equipped with two rows of lethal-looking, tiny teeth. It was restrained by a black rubber leash plugged into the wall to keep it from running amok through downtown Ishpeming. He pressed the switch, and the clippers sprang to life with a snarl like a power saw chomping through a log, the teeth disappearing in a blur of motion.

The barber was almost totally bald. Was he cutting his own hair when the clippers went out of control?

The old man always cut my hair, and I'd gotten used to it. But he only used scissors and Sears and Roebuck hand-operated clippers, not something that was capable of making sawdust out of your skull.

I made a last-ditch appeal to my mother who was sitting by the door looking disapprovingly at photographs of half-clad, female victims in the latest issue of *True Detective*.

"Pop always cuts my hair," I whimpered. "Can't we wait till he comes back?"

He pressed the switch, and the clippers sprang to life with a snarl like a power saw chomping through a log.

"When he comes back, he'll be so shaky that he'd whack off one of your ears. Shut up and let the barber finish."

The barber launched into his usual opening remarks on world politics. "Well, d'ya think we ought'a send foreign aid to Churchill t'help 'im beat the Nazis?"

I had no opinion.

Rivers of sweat ran down from my armpits, across my ribs, and soaked into the waistband of my underwear as we trudged up to the front entrance of the Mather Inn. The sun was low on the horizon, but the heat of the day still lingered, and I had lost three pounds since leaving the house in the new wool suit.

My hair was radiating an overwhelming bouquet of Wildroot Creme Oil from the barber shop. It had a fatal attraction for mosquitoes. Several of them were hopelessly glued fast to the viscous combination of hair and hair oil, uttering last-gasp whines on top of my head.

My mother looked absolutely stunning in her navy-blue wool dress that she had worn to the Bethaney Lutheran Church every Sunday since I could remember. The veil attached to her hat covered her face, softening the surly expression she'd worn since yesterday when we heard about the old man's bender. She was carrying an A&P shopping bag filled with roast beef sandwiches, a thermos bottle of milk, and a large bunch of green grapes. One should always have an ample food supply whenever travelling by train, in the event it jumped the tracks and you had a long wait for the rescue team. Since we were going directly to the railroad depot after supper, she was lugging the shopping bag into the Mather Inn.

We went through the main entrance into a lobby softly lit from the glow of an enormous glass chandelier. I sank ankle-deep into a plush, pearl-gray rug. The dining room was off to the right—still fairly empty since it was only five-thirty in the afternoon.

Arne Rouhomaki was standing at the dining room door in a swanky wine-colored jacket with a matching tie. Arne lived over on Third Street and had just been released from high school. His face lit up with a false-hearted smile as he walked over.

"Good evening. May I help you?"

I had never heard Arne talk like that before. He must have taken a summer-school course in English.

"A small table for the two of us for supper," my mother said.

Arne cast a quick, furtive glance at the A&P shopping bag. "Uh...do you have a dinner reservation?"

"No."

"Well...I'm sorry, you have to have a reservation..."

She looked over his shoulder into the dining room. "Listen, I see plenty of empty tables in there. Do you want me to go over to your house tomorrow and tell your mother that you wouldn't give us a table for supper?"

Arne nervously shot a glance toward the registration desk on the other side of the lobby, searching for reinforcements, the pimples on his forehead gleaming in the chandelier light. "Uh...well...we may have an extra table..."

We followed him into the huge dining room with its sea of sparkling-white tablecloths adorned with heavy plates, gleaming silverware, and tall, stemmed glasses. My heart pounded with the excitement of the moment. Up to now, my experience in eating out had been limited to hamburgers at the Busy Bee Hamburger Stand and hot fudge sundaes in Newberry's. I had never been in a restaurant where you didn't sit at a counter.

Arne headed for a table near the kitchen door, but my mother thwarted that idea. "This one over here next to the window will be fine," she said, pointing at one of the prime tables in the room.

Arne opened his mouth to say something, but thought better of it and seated us at the window table. He handed us menus. "A waiter will be with you shortly," he said and scurried back to the safety of his post at the door.

I opened up the menu. "What's this?"

"That's a menu—the food they serve here."

I scanned the lists on both sides of the menu. "We're gonna eat all this?"

"Blockhead—you pick something out, and they bring it to you."

"Do they have hamburgers?"

"You don't order hamburgers here. Look, put that down—I'll pick something out for you."

"A place this ritzy outta have hamburgers." I fingered the silverware at my place setting. "Look, they goofed up an' gave me too many knives, forks, an' spoons."

"One of the forks is for your salad, and the other is for your meat and vegetables. The little knife is for the butter, and the sharp one is for the meat. One spoon is for coffee, which you're not gonna get, and the other one is for dessert."

"Do I hafta remember all that?"

A waiter in a snowy-white, close-fitting jacket walked up. "Good evening," he purred, looking at my mother. "Would you care for wine or a cocktail?"

That was not a smart opening remark. She nailed him with her best indignant-Lutheran stare. "Do I look like the type of person who drinks cocktails?"

He digested the question for a second, glanced at the A&P shopping bag by her chair, and said, "Would you like a beer?"

"LOOK, CAN'T YOU JUST BRING US SOME DECENT FOOD LIKE A GOOD CHRISTIAN?"

The waiter recoiled from the verbal blast, and people at other tables turned to look. Attempting to recover his regal composure, he blurted, "Of course. Would you like to order now?"

My mother gave him an order for the both of us, and he scuttled off for the kitchen.

I looked out the window toward the street. "Hey, Ma, there's Kippy!" I jumped up and waved both hands. "HEY, KIPPY!"

She leaned over, grabbed one of my arms and hissed. "Sit down and keep quiet. You don't yell like that in a nice restaurant."

I blinked disappointedly at the salad the waiter placed in front of me. "Is this all we get?"

"That's just the salad," my mother said. "They'll bring you the rest when you finish that."

I never cared much for salads, but my mother was convinced that The Good Lord created vegetables for a reason, and that was to keep the planet regular. "Celery is cheaper than Castoria," she would say, plunking down a mammoth bowl of lettuce, sliced carrots, celery, and raw rutabagas on the kitchen table. Actually, I always thought Castoria tasted better than celery.

"Why don' they bring it all at once so you kin mix it up on the plate?" I had found by experimentation that raw vegetables became more palatable when you pushed them into the mashed potatoes and gravy to soften them up and give them a good gravy taste.

"They're still cooking the rest of the food."

"Iz that 'cause they didn't know we were comin'?"

"Just eat your salad."

"Kin I save the salad fer Teddy? He'll like it." My dog, Teddy, would eat anything, although raw vegetables tended to give him gas.

"Eat it and keep quiet!" she snapped. "At these prices, the dog isn't gonna see any of this food."

I inspected the object impaled on my fork. "Is this a baby meatball?"

"It's a Swedish meatball."

"Why izzit so small?" My mother made meatballs, but they were the size of baseballs, and one or two would put you away for the rest of the day. These were strictly bush-league meatballs, looking like lumpy, brown marbles. There were eight of them on the plate to compensate for their puniness.

"That's the way the Swedes make them. Just eat them and don't ask so many questions...and take your elbows off the table."

"But if I don't keep my elbows on the table, the suit sleeves come over my fingers, an' I'll get 'em in the gravy." This was indeed true. With my elbows on the table, the huge coat sleeves of my new jumbo suit were like two smokestacks on a battleship.

The meatballs were OK but didn't measure up to the ones my mother made. I was hoisting the last one to my mouth when it fell off the fork into the left coat sleeve of my suit. I quickly put the fork down and peered into the sleeve, but all I could see was my pencil-thin arm disappearing into the darkness.

"What are you doing?" my mother asked.

"Oh...uh...nothin'. I wuz jus' lookin' at my new suit."

I took my left elbow off the table, and hung my arm down at my side. Looking down at the rug, I shook my arm a couple of times. The meatball didn't come out.

This was bad. If I told my mother what had happened, she'd be yelling about my elbows on the table until I was seventy years old.

"I said, do you want some dessert?"

She was talking to me. I quickly looked up. "What?"

"Do you want dessert? They got your favorite—blueberry pie a la mode." She leaned over the table and looked closely at me. "Are you all right?"

"Oh...yeah...I'm OK."

I didn't enjoy the blueberry pie a la mode as much as I normally would since I was obsessed with the mystery meatball. Where did it go? Would it come rolling out of my sleeve in front of my mother when I least expected it?

After dessert, she paid the bill at the cash register with dollar bills, fifty-cent pieces, quarters, dimes, and nickels. Looking back at our table, I saw the waiter staring resignedly at his fourteen-cent tip.

Walking to the railroad depot, I was sure I felt the meatball crawling up my arm toward my armpit. I shook my left arm again several times.

"*What* is wrong with you?" my mother barked. "I think your father's drinking's got you twitchy. I'm gonna talk to the school nurse when school starts in September."

"No—no, I'm OK—really." The last time she talked to the school nurse, I was on cod-liver oil for two weeks.

Kippy was waiting at the depot when we arrived. Enjoying a good meal that she didn't have to cook had put my mother in an expansive mood, and she let Kippy come on board the Four Hundred with us to inspect the inside. He and I ran through several of the coaches, bouncing experimentally on empty seats to find the very best ones for the journey, then dashed down to the dining car to make certain that the black men were still on board. But after only a few minutes, the conductor made all the spectators get off and we were on our way.

With a gentle jerk, the Four Hundred started moving out of the Ishpeming depot. I pressed my nose against the coach window and waved wildly at Kippy standing despondently on the platform.

The streamliner picked up speed as we passed through east Ishpeming. Here we go, I said to myself, with the confidence of one who was a high-velocity expert. We'll be up to three hundred miles an hour in no time; those telephone poles will be nothing but one solid blur. My mother'll probably get scared and grab my hand—I'll just pat her hand and tell her it's all right.

The Four Hundred started to slow down.

Panic welled up in my throat. I turned to my mother. "What's wrong with the train?"

"*Nothing's* wrong with it. We're coming into Negaunee."

Negaunee already? The ride was over before the Four Hundred even got going! "Kin we stay on the train till the next stop?" I begged.

She grabbed my hand and picked up the A&P shopping bag. "C'mon. If you think I'm gonna miss Jack Benny just to take a ride to the Wisconsin border, you gotta another think coming."

"Lansing," I said.

Dr. IQ, the famous radio quiz show host standing on the stage of the Vista Theater in Negaunee, threw his hands into the air. "That's right! Lansing is the capital of Michigan. You've just won a million dollars! Usher, give that boy his money."

An usher in a blue uniform came down the theater aisle and stopped at my seat. He had two A&P shopping bags crammed full of dollar bills. I jumped up, grabbed the handles of the shopping bags, and had started running up the aisle toward the exit when Dr. IQ spoke up.

"Hold it a minute, young man. I must explain that it's the policy of this quiz show to lay down rules that all winners must follow. In the case of new millionaires, you must use part of that money to buy a new suit every day, get a haircut and steam bath every morning, and always have dinner in a fancy restaurant. That shouldn't be too hard to do, should it?" The stage lights lit up Dr. IQ's smarmy smile.

I turned around, walked back to my seat, and gave the shopping bags to the usher. "Keep yer money. I wouldn't do that every day for *ten* million dollars."

The smile faded from Dr. IQ's sweaty face. He jumped off the stage and ran up the aisle to my seat. "You don't understand...you have no choice about the money. You're a millionaire now, and you *must* do those things every day. You have no choice!" He shook me by the shoulders violently...

I opened my eyes. People were getting up from their seats and heading up the aisle. My mother was shaking me by the shoulder. "You fell asleep halfway through the movie. I guess I kept you up too long."

"Whaa...wha happened t'Jack Benny?"

"The movie's over. C'mon, time to go home."

My brain started to unscramble by the time we got out on the street. "What time izzit?"

My mother was taking inventory of the contents of the A&P shopping bag. "Almost ten o'clock."

"What time does the Four Hundred go back to Ishpeming?"

"Four Hundred? The Four Hundred's almost to Milwaukee by now. Did you think we were going to ride on it both ways? We're gonna walk home."

I accepted this stoically as we headed off into the darkness. After all the other indignities that had been heaped on me today, a three-mile walk was penny-ante stuff.

Normally, the walk from Negaunee to Ishpeming wouldn't have been too bad. It was dark, but there were occasional street lights about every two or three hundred yards or so. And the gravel road had been recently graded, so most of the bigger rocks and holes were gone.

The thunderstorm made it a little tough, though.

My mother had the foresight to stash an umbrella in the shopping bag, but the gale-force wind that sprang up blew the rain sideways. The new wool suit had a definite affinity for water, soaking up the rain like a giant sponge. In no time at all, I weighed two hundred pounds.

For some perverse reason, I started to think about the missing meatball again, and sure enough, I felt it crawling up my biceps in search of more body heat. In a panic, I shook my arm, watching the mud puddles on the road carefully to see the splash if the meatball fell out.

"WILL YOU CUT THAT OUT?" my mother yelled above the drumming of the rain.

The A&P shopping bag, which had taken on the consistency of graham-cracker mush from the rain, gave up the ghost. The bottom fell out, and the roast beef sandwiches, the green grapes, and the thermos bottle plopped into the mud.

How could a day which held so much promise go so utterly wrong? How could anybody wind up being so miserable just trying to spend money?

"Ma, we ain't millionaires, huh?"

My mother was cramming the waxed-paper-wrapped roast beef sandwiches and green grapes into her bulging purse and wiping off the thermos bottle with her hand. She straightened up and looked at me through rain-spattered glasses. "Of *course* we're millionaires. We're just out here in the dark, playing in the mud, because the chauffeur had to get the oil changed in the limousine tonight."

"What's a lim'zine?"

"It'll be a long time before you see one—here, carry the thermos bottle."

We slogged on toward Ishpeming. I carefully dodged the larger mud puddles to keep my good shoes from getting too soaked.

"Ma, why does pop go on benders?"

"I dunno," she sighed. "He gets so sick afterward it almost kills him. I guess it's because he works so hard at farming potatoes and doesn't have much to show for it. He just has to cut loose every once in a while. Always comes back sober though, I'll say that much for him. Some take it out on their wives and kids—he just goes off on a bender. Could be worse, I guess."

"I really like him a lot the rest of the time."

"Me, too," she said. "When he comes back he'll be OK for another year."

"Las' year when he came back from his bender he took me out to the Marquette Airport to see the Ford Tri-Motor airplane land, an' then we gotta hot fudge sundae at Newberry's. He wuz pretty nice."

"It's called guilt," she said.

The thunderstorm passed just about the time we sloshed up to our house. The light was on in my parents' bedroom.

A wave of relief swept over me. "Hey, pop's home."

"Yeah, so I see."

"You're not gonna hit 'im with the truss, are ya?"

She let out a long sigh. "No, I don't think so. I'm pretty tired, and my aim'd be bad. Besides, we spent more money than he did, and I'm gonna have to figure out how I'm gonna explain *that* to him and still stay mad."

"The next time he goes on a bender, let's not go out an' try to spend money, OK?"

She smiled for the first time in two days. "OK."

I followed her into the kitchen, both of us dripping water on the linoleum floor. Teddy had been sleeping under the table. He got up, yawned and stretched, and came over to me sleepily wagging his tail.

I was taking off my soggy suit coat when disaster struck. The meatball sprang out from its hiding place and fell on the floor.

With a lightning move that would have caught Joe Louis flat-footed, Teddy snatched it with his jaws on the first bounce and swallowed it whole. My mother, five feet away, was taking off her hat with its soggy veil and missed the whole thing.

I leaned over and whispered in Teddy's furry ear. "See, I *tol'ja* I'd bring ya somethin' from the Mather Inn."

Stella Dallas and the 50L6 Caper

ILL—WAUUU—KEEE!…MILL—WAUUU—KEEE!… AAALLL OUUUT FORRRR MILWAUKEE!" The ticket punch dangling from the conductor's belt was as shiny as his blue serge Milwaukee Road uniform. He tapped me on the shoulder as he passed my seat. "This is where you get off, son."

I knew that! Did he think I was some kind of runny-nosed runt who had never ridden on a train before? Jeez! I was ten and a half years old!

September 1943—I was reluctantly coming back to Milwaukee, where my parents and I lived during World War II. I had just spent my summer vacation with my grandmother in the Upper Peninsula of Michigan, fishing for trout, keeping the rat population at the town dump under control with my trusty slingshot, and getting an intensive course in sexually explicit obscenities from my buddy, Mutt Hukala. When it came to swearing, the Upper Peninsula kids were light years ahead of my new friends in Milwaukee. With all the new rotten words now in my vocabulary, I was sure to nail down a high-ranking post in the Kilbourn Street Gremlins, a Milwaukee gang I had joined last spring.

I grabbed my cardboard suitcase from the rack above the seat and picked up the bulky A&P paper shopping bag containing my food supply. This morning, my grandmother had sliced up the better part of a cow, making roast beef sandwiches to keep me from starving to death on the train. It was a message to my mother that I had been fed well during the summer. The train could have kept going to Rio de Janeiro, and I would have had enough left to pass out roast beef sandwiches to the Brazilians.

I spilled out onto the depot platform with the rest of the plaid-shirted travellers from the North, dragging my suitcase and the bag of sandwiches. Spotting the old man standing next to my mother, I pressed through the crowd. As I neared, I could see he was holding a large box with a picture of an airplane on it.

It was the deluxe Revell airplane model kit of the Lockheed P-38 Lightning!

I had been lusting after that model since last fall. With a five-foot wing span, it contained the most minute details of the real fighter plane. The machine-gun barrels in the nose even had air-vent holes, which was not something found in your run-of-the-mill airplane models.

Why would the old man buy it now? When I confessed to him that it cost four dollars and fifty cents, he had laughed like hell and said that if he was going to spend that kind of money, he'd toss in a few extra bucks and buy a real airplane.

My mother hugged me and handed over the paper bag she had been carrying. Butcher Block hamburgers—with fried onions—my most favorite food in the world!—What was going on?—Had they figured out that they just couldn't afford to keep me any longer and sold me to an adoption agency?— Were the presents just to make me feel better about it?

I looked up at the old man who had a wide, somewhat superficial, grin on his face. "Is there sumthin' wrong?" I asked him.

"Wrong? Whaddaya mean?"

"The airplane model that I wanted...the hamburgers...there's somethin' wrong, ain't there?"

As we headed for the nearest bus stop, a couple of stray dogs locked onto the scent of the roast beef sandwiches and the hamburgers. The old man aimed a half-hearted kick at the nearest one. "Well...there ain't any school tomorrow."

"Y'mean school don't start tomorrow? An' *that's* what's wrong?" I breathed a long sigh of relief, reached into the bag, and jubilantly wrapped a hand around a greasy Butcher Block hamburger.

Butcher Block hamburgers were truly delicious, but the rationing of meat during the war made the ingredients the subject of much debate. The old man said that, being an ex-lumberjack, he recognized sawdust when he tasted it, and that furthermore, he had spotted a couple of old horses tied up behind the Butcher Block hamburger stand one day. I always looked behind the stand before I bought a Butcher Block hamburger.

In a serious tone, my mother picked up the conversation. "They've got a lot of polio in Milwaukee. We read in the paper this morning that they made it an official epidemic."

Polio. The dreaded disease that no one could find a cure for—even FDR had caught it. It usually struck children, leaving them crippled. Of course, at age ten and a half, it wasn't high on my list of things to worry about. I bit into the aromatic Butcher Block hamburger.

"So...with no school, I guess summer vacation jus' lasts a li'l longer."

She put her hand on my shoulder. "Well...there's more...they've put a quarantine on all the kids in the city. In fact, we've got to go straight home."

"What's a quarantine?"

"You're not gonna be able to leave our yard until they call it off."

Suddenly, the Butcher Block hamburger stuck in my throat. "Oh."

Wally Schultz, my friend from next door, was sitting on his front steps, glumly holding his chin in his hands, and looking over at me through the picket fence between our yards. "What ya gonna do durin' the quarantine?"

"Put the P-38 model together, I guess. That'll take me three weeks, at least. After that, I dunno."

"Ya think it'll last longer'n three weeks?"

"Prob'ly. My old man sez th'polio is goin' around pretty fast. We might be stuck in our yards till they find a cure."

Wally's eyes widened in near panic. "That might be years!"

The whole subject was starting to depress me. "Yeah...d'ya think when I get old 'nough, the old man'll bring me some beer with the model airplanes? A course, by then, we prob'ly won't have room for any more airplanes in the apartment anyhow."

"JERRRRRRRYYYYYYY!...SUPPERRRRRRR!" My mother had her head stuck out of our tiny third-floor kitchen window, announcing the evening meal. I got up from the front steps and took my pack of candy cigarettes from my shirt pocket. This was a vice I had acquired at the age of seven, and though I had tried to quit a couple of times, candy cigarettes were a tough habit to break. I stuck one in the corner of my mouth like James Cagney did in the prison movies and swaggered over to the picket fence.

"Well, that's chow call. See ya here in th'yard, same time tomorrow?"

Wally narrowed his eyes and pursed his lips in the best George Raft style. "Yeh, same time tomorrow."

"SU—PER SUDS!...SU—PER SUDS!...LOTS MORE SUDS WITH
        SU—PER
                SU—   —DS!"
              —UU—

Our wooden floor-model Zenith radio blared out the jingle beside the card table where I was launching into the assembly of the Lockheed P-38 the next morning. The quarantine was going to be a lonely vigil since both of my parents had jobs: the old man putting Army trucks together at International Harvester and my mother sewing brassieres for the Women's Army Corps. It promised to be a balmy September day, and I had our electric fan running to dissipate the heat generated by the fifty-eight vacuum tubes in the radio. The three-and-a-half-foot-high Zenith was the old man's pride and joy. A couple of years before, after a particularly profitable potato crop, he had convinced my mother that we needed the best radio that money could buy. It had a back-lit tuning dial about the size of a dinner plate with a mind-boggling array of frequency numbers. Laboriously, the old man kept reading the owner's manual, and one night, which will go down in the historical annals of our household, he discovered that the radio had shortwave. He had been fiddling with the knobs and tuning dial when a blast of Spanish came out of the speaker, ending with the electrifying words "Havana, Cuba."

"HEY! I GOT CUBA ON TH'RADIO!"

So we sat there and listened attentively to a fifteen-minute news broadcast in Spanish, a language in which none of us were too well versed, and enjoyed every minute. From then on, every night was a new adventure to see what exotic ports-of-call we could pull in on shortwave. After hearing a radio offer, my mother toyed briefly with the idea of sending away to Del Rio, Texas, for a two-foot-high, plug-in statue of Jesus Christ that would cast a warm glow in the dark to guide you safely through the night. For an extra dollar, you could get an optional, rotating halo. Finally, she decided against it, figuring that it might be a trifle flashy for a Lutheran household.

When we moved to Milwaukee, the old man had lovingly crated up the radio, and it now held a place of honor and prominence in our small living room.

Organ music wafted out of the lone speaker.

> And now, we once again bring you the story of a woman born in a small mining town in Minnesota. The story that asks the question—Can this midwestern girl, who was raised in poverty, find happiness married to a wealthy, educated socialite from New York City?

What kind of dumb question was that? I was an expert on poverty in small mining towns, and all the single women I ever knew would jump at the chance of latching onto a rich guy from New York City, no matter how far he got in school. Even some of the married ones would give it some thought. If this woman was still asking herself the question about finding happiness, she obviously had taken too many shots to the head from iron ore chunks when she was a kid. I twisted the radio dial.

But all the stations had the same fare. Briefly, I eavesdropped on the romantic entanglements in "The Right to Happiness," "John's Other Wife," "Ma Perkins," "The Romance of Helen Trent," and several others. In sheer desperation I switched over to shortwave to see if I could pick up some rumba music from Havana. I would have even settled for some soul-searing gospel from Del Rio, Texas, but due to some atmospheric quirk over Lake Michigan, the shortwave reception was terrible. I went back to the AM band and surrendered to the trials and tribulations of the next fifteen-minute daytime serial, or soap opera as my mother called them, while I started to assemble the ribs of the Lockheed P-38.

In Morgansville, Helen is contemplating the odd turn of events which revealed to her the fact that her brother Brent was working as a field hand in the avocado orchards in central California instead of taking the accountant job in Tyler, as she had been led to believe, while Brent himself, having moved to Fresno, has had a chance encounter with Alicia, who reminded him that he had never replied to Louise's letter, which declared her undying love for him...

I put down my Exacto knife and stared at the radio. I hadn't followed that at all. Had I left the tube of airplane glue open too long? Do women actually plan supper and keep track of stories like that at the same time? Could it be my mother was right when she claimed that women were smarter than men?

Naw...I'd just have to pay closer attention.

A week dragged by, and except for brief daily visits with Wally through the picket fence, I spent my time assembling the P-38 model while listening to the soap operas. Slowly but surely, I started to pick up the threads of the convoluted plots. I found out that Anthony had secretly taken leave from the Army to fly to New York City to seek consultation with an eye specialist regarding "Young Widder Brown's" sudden blindness. I deduced why the twenty-five-year-old oil painting hanging on Mr. Dunbar's wall, depicting a World War I Army nurse, bore such an eerie resemblance to Mary Noble, "Backstage Wife." I agonized with Peter Marlow on "The Guiding Light," when he summoned up his courage to go to the Bar Association to admit to a courtroom impropriety he had committed seven years earlier.

My vocabulary was expanding by leaps and bounds. One night at the supper table I turned to the old man, who was shoveling in the hash made from last Sunday's pot roast.

"Pop, what does disbarment mean?"

His forkful of hash stopped in midair. He thoughtfully scratched his chin with his free hand as he rummaged through his brain for an answer.

"Well, it's like when yur granmother went down to the Jack Pine Bar an' tol' the bartender that if he ever served your Uncle Arnold another drink, she'd bust an axe handle over his head. That's disbarment!"

A few days later, one of the more avant-garde radio dramas triggered an even more intriguing supper-table discussion.

"Pop, what's a harem?"

The old man smiled as he chewed his fried Spam; he knew the right answer to this one. "It's a place in a palace where the Arab sheiks keep all their wives."

"All their wives? How many do they have?"

"Some a them got dozens, I guess."

"Dozens? Ain't that illegal?"

"The laws are prob'ly different over there, and 'sides, rich people kin do whatever th'hell they want, I guess."

"But why would a guy want dozens of wives?"

"Tha's a real good question. It mus' cost a bundle t'feed 'em."

"Maybe the sheik tells 'em t'go out an' get jobs t'bring home a pay-check."

"I don't think he does that," he said.

"Boy, I think dozens of wives are too many, don't you?"

"Kid, somedays one is too many."

My mother rapped him across the head with a wooden salad spoon.

The weeks trudged on into October, and the quarantine showed no signs of letting up. I finished the Lockheed P-38 model and hung it from the antiquated light fixture in our living room. By now, all of my fingers were about one-quarter-inch longer, since they had acquired a thick, impene-trable layer of model airplane cement. The old man immediately went out and bought me another model, a Consolidated B-24 Liberator. This one was a four-engine job and even larger than the P-38 model. On one hand I was ecstatic about getting these expensive models to build, but it could only mean one thing: the old man thought that the polio quarantine was going to be around for quite awhile.

But a strange thing was happening—I was adjusting to the confine-ment. I had settled into a nice, comfortable routine where after breakfast I would lay out my model airplane assembly line on the card table in the middle of the living room and fire up the radio. I had compiled a marathon sequence of preferred soap operas that ran for about six straight hours. Day after day I listened in on my troup of well-meaning featherbrains drifting in over the radio waves. I yelled advice into the radio speaker whenever they were on the brink of doing something really stupid. At the age of ten and a half, I had become an expert on broken marriages, unbounded deceit, shattered careers, and unrequited love. Like all addicts, I didn't admit it to myself, but I had become hooked on soap operas.

One program emerged head and shoulders above the rest—"Stella Dallas." Stella devoted her middle-aged years to extricating her married daughter and wealthy in-laws from various perilous predicaments brewed up by bad acquaintances. How these well-bred socialites could run into so many rotten people was a constant source of amazement to me. I liked Stella. She had been raised in a mill town, said "ain't" a lot, and didn't use four-syllable words that taxed my fifth-grade education. She had a take-charge personality and didn't put up with any guff from anybody. She must have had a Swiss bank account which she dipped into occasionally to provide whatever resources were necessary to foil the latest sinister scheme.

But one morning Wally threw a monkey wrench into the works. During a candy cigarette break at the picket fence, as I patiently explained a blossoming love rectangle on "Young Widder Brown," Wally remarked in a bored, dry tone, "Why'da'ya keep listenin' to that crap for? Don'cha know those programs are fer women? The quarantine mus' be turnin' ya into a tutti-frutti sissy!"

Tutti-frutti sissy? Tutti-frutti sissy?

Wally cackled good-naturedly at his own feeble wit and immediately dismissed the topic by launching into his latest half-baked scheme for pulling off a daring escape from Milwaukee. I went back upstairs and sat down at the card table, but he had planted a neurotic seed in my mind. Was the quarantine changing me? Were the soap operas turning me into a girl? OK, I'd quit listening to them. I didn't turn on the radio for the rest of the day.

But...by the next morning, the silence was closing in on me like a coffin. "Stella Dallas" was coming on at ten o'clock! After twisting the knob on the Zenith so hard that it almost came off in my hand, I calmed down as the organ music filtered into the room. Fifteen minutes a day of "Stella Dallas" couldn't possibly turn somebody into a tutti-frutti sissy.

One Friday morning in late October I was ready to mount the wings on the fuselage of the B-24 and eager to find out how Stella was going to rescue her daughter Laurel from the clutches of an intoxicated industrialist who had her cornered in one of the upper bedrooms of his Long Island mansion. It promised to be a day of high adventure. I turned on the Zenith.

PUZZZ.....POPPP!!!..... ZZZTTT!!!

A thin trail of acrid smoke wafted out of the back of the radio cabinet—the Zenith had blown a tube!

Jumping up, I wrestled the radio around to look inside. Peering into the forest of tubes, I spotted one that was prominently blackened. Yup, it was the 50L6 tube again. Ever since the old man had bought the radio, it had a penchant for blowing this one particular tube. He had already replaced it three times, once since we had moved to Milwaukee.

My heart started to rap under my breastbone. What was I going to do? My parents were at work, and as a matter of fact, I was probably the only one here in the whole apartment house. I'd been to Walgreen's Drug Store with the old man when he last replaced the tube, so I knew where to get a new one. But I couldn't leave the yard because of the quarantine.

I was going to miss "Stella Dallas!"

Pacing feverishly around the small living room, I groped for a solution. Should I take a chance and run to Walgreen's for a tube? Weeks ago, my mother had made a big point of telling me that the cops were picking up kids who were roaming the streets, breaking the quarantine. What was the sentence for breaking quarantine? A year in jail? Two?

In less than an hour, "Stella Dallas" was going to be on the air. How was she going to deal with the drunken industrialist out on Long Island?

Then...staring at the old man's reading glasses sitting on the arm of the sofa, I knew I had the answer—a disguise.

If I did this carefully, I could pass as a little old man and get to the drug store and back. Let's see...I'd need to put on my suit and tie, find my church shoes, and of course, the final touch would be the old man's dark, felt fedora and his reading glasses. No kid ever wore glasses like that.

Aha! I ran into my parents' bedroom and opened the closet door. Yeah—there it was: the old man's wooden cane. He had a trick knee and needed the cane from time to time. I grabbed the curved handle to try it on for size. The head of the cane came up to my chest—too long—digging further into the closet, I found the old man's tool chest with a small saw inside. I went into the kitchen, put the cane across a kitchen chair and sawed five inches off the bottom. He'd probably never even notice the difference.

I put on a white shirt and my only suit, found my necktie, only then remembering that my mother always tied the knot for me. Time was running short, so I wrapped the tie around my neck and put a double granny knot in it. Boy, that didn't look right at all—the knot made one of the shirt collar tips stick straight out, but it would have to do.

The old man's reading glasses slid right down my nose and fell on the carpet when I tried them on. By now my brain was hitting on all cylinders; I ran into the bathroom, cut two strips from our roll of white adhesive tape, and taped the earpieces of the glasses to the hair behind my ears. The glasses bounced on my nose when I walked, but I could look right over the lenses, just like the old man.

His hat was also a problem. He had an extra-large noggin, and the fedora came down over my ears. From my mother's bureau I got out the big, blue Kotex box I had seen in there. I only had a hazy idea of what the pads were for, but she always had a plentiful supply. Using safety pins, I pinned four of the pads to the sweatband of the hat. Great—the hat fit just fine! I could put the pads back in the box when I was done.

With cane in hand, I checked myself over in the mirror.

It was truly amazing—I had aged forty years in just fifteen minutes. With this disguise, I could easily go over to one of the taverns on Clybourn Street and order a beer. I dismissed that idea since time was running short. Walgreen's was only two blocks away—I'd be in and out of there before anybody was the wiser. After shaking a fistful of coins out of my savings bank, I went out the door.

Wally was sitting on his front steps when I came out of the apartment house. His eyes bugged out, and he jumped to his feet.

"HEY! YER MAKIN' A BREAK FER IT! WHAT A GREAT DISGUISE!"

I shook the cane at him and whispered. "Wally...shaddup! I'll be right back." I started to scurry down the street.

But Wally wasn't listening. He hopped up and down excitedly on the top step of the porch. "GOOD LUCK! I HOPE YA MAKE IT BACK TO MICHIGAN! AN' DON' WORRY! I WON'T SQUEAL ON YA FER ANYTHIN'!"

There are those of us who go through life coloring between the lines and others who just eat the crayons. Wally was definitely a crayon-eater.

I went up Eighteenth Street and turned on Wisconsin Avenue. Stooping my shoulders over to display my old age and tapping the cane on the sidewalk at intervals, I shuffled down the street. It was a crisp autumn morning with the leaves turning color on the trees lining Wisconsin Avenue, but the sweat rolled down from my armpits, soaking my shirt.

I made it to Walgreen's without incident, walked in, and went to the back of the store where they kept the radio tubes next to the pharmacy. The reading glasses were gently bouncing up and down on my nose as I approached a balding man wearing a starched white pharmacist's jacket.

He put both palms flat on the counter and gave me a stern look. "Young man, you're not supposed to be here. Don't you know the quarantine's still on?"

Wasn't I fooling anybody? My mind raced. "Yeah, I know...but I had to come. My father's at work, an' my mother's pretty sick an' can't get out of bed. She sent me here to get her somethin'."

His look changed to one of concern. "Oh? Have you called a doctor?"

"We don't have a phone, an' besides, we don't know any doctors. We just moved into town."

He picked up the receiver on the black telephone on the counter. "There's a doctor right over here on Seventeenth Street. Let me give him a call."

I put up my hand. "No...my mother told me 'xactly what she needs. This's happened to her before."

"What does she want?"

I mentally counted the coins in my pocket. "A tin of aspirin'll make her right as rain."

"She can't get out of bed, and all she wants is aspirin?"

"Yeah...that'll do it all right."

He reached to a shelf behind him and put a tin of aspirin on the counter. "Are you sure you don't want me to call the doctor?"

"Nope! I'll jus' slip her a couple a these aspirin, an' she'll be up an' around in an hour."

He bent over and looked at me closely. "Son, are those your own glasses you're wearing?"

"Yeah, I got bad eyes from workin' on too many model airplanes." Putting a nonchalant look on my face, I pulled out the 50L6 radio tube out of my pocket. "Oh, by the way, do you have this kind'a tube? My mother'll feel a lot better if I can get our radio workin' an' she can listen to 'Stella Dallas.'"

I skulked out of Walgreen's with my ill-gotten purchase and headed for home.

"Hey, kid...hold up there!"

I whipped my head around and saw a cop looking hard at me from about fifty feet away. OH, GAWD! Clutching the 50L6, I took off for Eighteenth Street like a jack rabbit.

My heart hammered as I dashed up Wisconsin Avenue. I knew that the cop could never catch me at the rate I was going, but as I neared Seventeenth Street, all of a sudden my legs turned to jelly—those weeks of sitting at the card table had taken their toll on my leg muscles. I started to wobble on the sidewalk and had to slow down. A vision snapped into my head with startling clarity...

Two cons are standing in the prison yard and one of them is pointing at me. "Hey, Rocky, that ten-and-a-half-year-old kid standing over at th'wall, smokin' candy cigarettes—what's he in for?"

Clutching the 50L6, I took off for Eighteenth Street like a jack rabbit.

"They caught 'im breakin' the polio quarantine."

"Izzat so? I really hate kids who do that! How many years they give 'im?"

"Two."

"Only two? An' they give me seven fer only robbin' a bank! Let's go beat the hell outta him."

"Sounds like a good idea."

Grunting with exertion, I willed my legs to keep moving. My eyes bulged as I staggered down the sidewalk.

Suddenly, a gust of wind off Lake Michigan blew the hat off of my head, and it sailed out into the middle of Wisconsin Avenue. The old man's good fedora! With a surge of adrenaline, I veered off the curb and scampered after it. Tires screeched and horns blared, but I had to get that hat back! It was lying there in the eastbound lane, and I thought I had a chance to get it—

An eastbound bus flattened it with one of its tires.

When the bus passed, I scooped up the pancaked hat, dashed to the opposite curb, and kept on running up to Eighteenth Street. Breathlessly, I lurched up to the apartment house. Wally was still on his front porch, and his face dropped a mile when he saw me.

"AAWWW! YA CAME BACK! WHAD'JA COME BACK FOR? I THOUGHT YOU WUZ BUSTIN' OUT!"

"Shaddup, Wally!"

In the apartment, I inspected the fedora. The brim and flattened crown had a wide set of tire tracks across them. The Kotex pads also had tire tracks but not as bad as the hat, so I brushed them off as best I could and put them back in the blue box. I pushed the hat back into some kind of shape, but no matter what I tried, I couldn't get the tire tracks out of the felt. What was the old man gonna do when he saw that? It was his good hat that he only wore for state occasions such as weddings and funerals. Another vision of the near future focused in my mind's eye:

> The Lutheran minister is standing by the open grave delivering a solemn farewell address:
>
> "We are gathered here today to ask the Lord to receive the soul of this young man who has left this earth under the most mysterious of circumstances..."
>
> My mother is crying, and the old man is standing next to her, poker-faced in his dark-blue suit. On his head is the dark, felt fedora, complete with tire tracks.

I put the fedora way in back of the top shelf in the closet, hoping that it would be a good long time before he had to use it. Maybe with luck, it would be at my wedding, and I could make a run for it with my wife and go and live with her parents.

The double granny knot in the necktie had become firmly set during the run, and since I couldn't get it up over my head, I had to cut it off with scissors. I would have to put on a look of pure innocence when my mother started looking for it next Sunday.

The only part of the caper that wasn't a complete disaster was that I had managed to get a new 50L6 radio tube. I plugged it in the Zenith just in time to catch "Stella Dallas."

> We now join Stella as she discusses strategy with her son-in-law, Dick Grosvenor, on how to go about rescuing Laurel from the Long Island mansion...
>
> "Dick, I think I know where to get an Army truck. We could mount some kind of battering ram on the front end and break down the front door."
>
> "But, Stella, neither of us has ever driven one of those big trucks."
>
> "Yeah...that's gonna be a problem all right..."

I rolled my eyes. Stella, for crissake, surely you can figure that one out after all I've been through for you today.

At five-thirty, the old man and my mother both came home at the same time.

"How'dit go today—anythin' exciting happen?" the old man asked.

I put on my best deadpan look. "What could be exciting, sitting around this apartment all day?"

My mother, standing behind him, brought her hand out from behind her back. Her face beamed as she handed me a sack of Butcher Block hamburgers.

I gave her a big grin. "Wow! Butcher Block hamburgers! What's the celebration?" I grabbed one out of the bag and bit into it.

"We heard it at work today. They announced that the number of polio cases has gone down far enough so that the quarantine is off, starting tomorrow."

I looked at her, dumbfounded. I could walk down the street without worrying about the cops? Even going to school would be a welcome change.

School! My gawd! If I'm in school on Monday, I won't find out how Stella gets into the Long Island mansion! The Butcher Block hamburger stuck in my throat.

"Wot tha hell..." the old man was sitting on the sofa. He had reached for his reading glasses, and one of the plastic earpieces stuck to his forefinger. It appeared to have some white sticky stuff on it.

"Good morning, class. My name is Miss Bridges, and I will be your sixth-grade teacher during this coming year. I know that all of you are very glad to be here this morning, now that the polio quarantine is over..."

The plump, pleasant-looking lady at the front of the classroom droned on and on. I didn't feel glad to be here at all. As a matter of fact, I was in a state of high agitation, suffering through my first day of "Stella Dallas" withdrawal.

Somebody tapped me on the shoulder. Murph, the top dog of the Kilbourn Street Gremlins, was sitting behind me. He had all the qualifications for leadership, being the biggest, meanest kid in our class, and knowing more about sex than any of the other members of the gang.

He whispered close to my ear. "Howzit goin'? Wha'ja do durin' the quarantine?"

I turned my head slightly. "Built model airplanes mostly...an' listened to the radio." I didn't dare tell him what programs I listened to.

"Yeah, I listened to th'radio a lot, too. Lemme show ya what else I was doin'." He rolled up his shirt sleeve, revealing a splendid ink "tattoo" on his forearm showing Hitler with a dagger through the heart, large drops of black blood trailing down to his wrist bone.

"Wow!" I whispered. "That's neat!"

"Yeah, but I gotta be careful t'keep it dry. I ain't washed this arm in three weeks. This's nuthin' though...I got one on my shoulder of the insignia of the U.S. Army Thirteenth Armored Division—in four colors. Hadda do it backwards using a mirror."

It was obvious that Murph was destined for great things in life.

At recess I was in the school yard shaking a candy cigarette out of the pack to soothe my nerves when I spotted Murph striding purposefully for the corner of the building. He had a smoldering candy cigarette hanging out of his mouth—the only kid I knew who actually lit them. I trotted after him.

"Hey, Murph. Show me the Armored Division insignia."

"Can't now...gotta go see a guy."

"Who ya gonna see?"

Furtively, he looked around and then leaned in close. "Look, I ain't got time t'stand here talkin'. If ya promise t'keep yer mouth shut, ya kin come with me."

I followed Murph around the corner of the school building to a door marked CUSTODIAN ONLY. Murph went in, and I slipped in after him. We were in the boiler room of the school. A burly, gray-haired guy in a brown uniform was sitting in an old wooden chair, smoking a pipe. He scowled at Murph.

"Dammit, Murph, I tol' ya you could come in here at recess, but I didn't mean fer ya t'bring all yer friends!"

Murph jerked his thumb at me. "He's OK...he's one a tha Gremlins."

The janitor reached over to a plastic table-model radio, turned it on, and adjusted the dial. Organ music filtered into the boiler room. I stopped in my tracks. That organ music...I KNEW THAT MUSIC—COULD IT BE?...

We give you now..."Stella Dallas." A true-to-life story of mother love and sacrifice...

With my mouth gaping open, I turned to Murph. "You listen to 'Stella Dallas'?"

Murph grabbed the front of my shirt and hoisted me up on my toes. "If ya breathe a word a this to anybody, I'll loosen every tooth in yer head!"

I dropped my voice to a reverent whisper. "Believe me, I ain't gonna tell a soul."

We now listen in on Stella and her son-in-law, Dick Grosvenor, as they sit in the cab of a two-and-a-half-ton Army truck in front of the Long Island mansion owned by wealthy industrialist, Reginald Scurdley...

GGGGGGGGGRRRRRRRR!!!!!!!!!!

"Gosh darn it, Stella, I can't seem to get the hang of getting this truck into first gear."

"I know, Dick. You're stripping the gears. I've just been reading the maintenance manual I found in the glove compartment, and I think I know how to double-clutch the transmission. You better let me take the wheel."

"Whatever you say, Stella..."

I sighed with contentment. Stella was back in control.

McGroarty's Choice

eez, what neat shoes!—completely white with large, fringed tongues that flopped out over the laces—spikes like baseball shoes. With a pair of those, I could nail down the right-field position on that softball team at my new school.

The bald-headed guy in the white golf shoes wasn't thinking about shoes or softball. He loomed over a golf ball on the practice tee of the driving range, convincing himself that he could hit it clear into the next state. Menacingly waggling the head of the golf club an inch or so behind the teed ball, he yanked the club back and up over his shoulder blades and with eyes bulging, took a vicious swing.

The ball zoomed out over the one-hundred-yard marker, but then, for no good reason, veered sharply off to the right, hit the ground about one hundred and fifty yards from where we were standing, and skittered into the woods.

Gawd! If I could throw a baseball with a curve like that, I could sign up with the Detroit Tigers right now at the age of twelve!

But apparently, Angus P. McGroarty, the golf pro giving the bald-headed guy a lesson, didn't think too much of putting a curve on a golf ball. He shrieked like a mad gorilla—a gorilla with a thick Scottish burr.

"Arre yurr ears filled up wi'wax? I kaep tellin' ye, ye hafta keep th'right elbow next t'tha body on th'swing. Yurr elbows'rre still flyin' oot like a chicken tryin' t'fly!" To emphasize his point, he stuck out his elbows and flapped them up and down several times.

Last winter I had read Dickens' *Christmas Carol*, and McGroarty fit my mental picture of Ebenezer Scrooge perfectly. McGroarty was about sixty years old with thinning, gray hair. With his pot belly and spindly legs, he looked like a pear held up by two pencils. The face was what really caught your eye—a big nose laced with spidery red veins, loose jowls, and extraordinary eyebrows with long white hairs jutting out over cold, deep-set gray eyes. He didn't have any lips—when he was talking, or more often, yelling, all you could see was the round, black hole of his open mouth. The rest of the time, his mouth was pinched tightly shut.

However, Scrooge wouldn't have been caught dead wearing McGroarty's clothes—an eye-jolting red, green, and black plaid sweater vest over a yellow woolen shirt, and baggy tweed knickers pulled down over brown and white Argyle socks. Golfers had worse taste in clothes than my old man.

McGroarty's imitation of a chicken was excellent, and I gave it an appreciative chuckle. He quickly turned and wilted me with a stony stare. "Who'rr'ya, y'pint-sized li'l bugger? Git th'hell outta here an' don'a bother people!" I scurried off.

May 1945—my parents had just landed jobs at the Green Knolls Country Club outside of Milwaukee. We had moved down from Michigan's Upper Peninsula a year earlier, living in downtown Milwaukee while my mother and the old man worked at defense jobs. The old man had a natural aversion to paying rent, so when he heard that the jobs at the Green Knolls clubhouse included room and board, he talked my mother into going out there.

Green Knolls was an exclusive private club. The old man said you had to own *at least* one of the Milwaukee breweries to join. I halfway believed him the first time I saw the clubhouse, a huge, rambling stone structure resembling a medieval castle. I had my own room, which was a major step up from sleeping on a Murphy bed in the living room of our small downtown apartment.

The club was open all year long for social functions, but the golf course had just opened for the season, giving me my first glimpse of Angus McGroarty. The old man had told me about McGroarty, who didn't get along with anyone and had the reputation of taking a jolt from a hip flask from time to time to endure the rigors of trying to teach the finer points of golf to the upper class. While some of the club members didn't appreciate McGroarty's bad temper, others felt that his reputation as being one of the best golfers in Scotland years back lent distinction to Green Knolls.

Until a week ago, I had never been on a golf course in my life. I knew nothing about the game except that you had to buy lots of equipment and wear funny-looking clothes. After watching McGroarty giving the lesson on the practice tee, it was clear there were plenty of things you could do wrong.

Living at Green Knolls would have been the ultimate ambition of any twelve-year-old boy from the woods of Upper Michigan—plush surroundings, your own room, good food—except there were problems. I was the *only* kid living there, and the country club was exactly that—a club out in the country. There wasn't a town for miles. The school I had just enrolled in was two miles away at the highway intersection, and kids were bussed in from neighboring farms.

So it was going to be a lonely summer. However, after watching McGroarty chew the tail off the bald-headed man, I figured there were worse things than being lonely—I could be forced to take golf lessons from McGroarty.

At dusk I stood watching the last group of golfers finish up on the eighteenth hole by the pro shop. One guy tried to roll the ball into the hole from a foot away and missed. The grass around the hole was the shortest and smoothest I'd ever seen, and anybody should have been able to do better than that. The guy who missed the shot thought so, too, because he swore a lot. From what I had seen so far, people didn't enjoy playing golf very much.

"Yer too small t'be a caddy, an' yer dressed too bummy t'be a member's boy, so who arre ye?"

The now-familiar voice barked out from behind me, and I jerked around to face McGroarty.

"I...live here. Ma an' pop work in the clubhouse. We got here a week ago."

"Be damned. So they'rre lettin' people wi' kids work here now. Well...ye hafta kaep off th'practice tee when I'm givin' lessons. I'll not hae ye laughin' at people who're payin' me ten dollars an hour t'instruct 'em on th'game a' golf."

"Ten dollars an hour? Holy...! I'm sorry, sir...I wasn't laughin' at the bald-heaa...the golfer, I was laughin' at you...I mean, I was laughin' at your chicken...I mean..."

McGroarty leaned forward and his alcohol-rich breath drove off the mosquitos that had started to buzz around my ears. "Ye don' hae' eny oother boys t'play with oot here?"

"No, sir..I guess I'm the only kid who lives here."

He thought about that for a moment. "Coome wi' me. I'll gie ye somethin' t'occupy yurr idle time, so ye won't be underrfoot." He turned and headed for the pro shop.

I followed him into the pro shop, through the front room with its dazzling display of Spaulding, Wilson, and McGregor clubs and bags, and into the back room. This was where the members' clubs were stored, cleaned, and repaired. A couple of McGroarty's workers were cleaning clubs in a washtub.

"Know enything aboot golf?" McGroarty asked me.

"Uh...not much."

"DON'A SAY 'NOT MOOCH' IF IT'S '*NOOTHIN*' YA MEAN!"

I snapped to attention. "I know nothing 'bout golf, sir."

McGroarty went to a corner of the room where there was a tangle of old, assorted clubs. He pulled one out of the heap. "I had this'un cut doown t'size fer a member's son who thoought he wanted t'learn th'game. Turned oot he didn' hae th'stomach furr th'lessons." He handed me the club.

It was a short club with a metal head pitted so badly it had turned a deep brown. It had a wooden shaft and dark handle made from smooth leather wound around the shaft. I grabbed the handle with both hands and waggled it back and forth, thereby committing my first golfing mistake.

"It's not a baseball bat, ye ninny! Ye mus' use an interlockin' grip wi' th'hands." McGroarty pried my right hand from the shaft and shoved the little finger between the index and middle fingers of my left hand. "Ye go now, and practice holdin' th'club like this till ye go t'bed. Tomorrow mornin' at seven, meet me oot in th'glade behind the shop an' I'll show ye how t'hit a golf ball."

"Uh...I don't have any money for golf lessons."

Nae'r mind aboot that. It'll be worth it t'kaep ye oot a m'hair."

"YURR LATE! I DON'A LIKE T'BE KEPT WAITIN'!"

"Sorry, sir."

McGroarty jerked a large gold watch out of a sweater-vest pocket. "If I say seven o'clock, I don'a mean two minutes past. I mean seven sharrp!"

"Yes, sir...Mr. McGroarty...kin I ask a question?"

McGroarty turned a canvas bag upside down, spilling a bunch of golf balls on the grass. "What is it?"

"This club you gave me...it has "MASHIE" stamped on the bottom. What's that mean?"

"It's th'name a th'club, as eny fool shoould know. It tells ye th'loft. Nowadays, th'manufacturers're boogerin' oop tha game an' only puttin' noombers on tha clubs—a sad state of affairs, indeed. The mashie is a noomber five iron. But that's the least a yurr worries right now. And another thing—I din'na *give* ye th'club. I'm lettin' ye *borrow* it until ye git tired a th'game, which'll be soon enough if I know enything aboot praesent-day, American yoong paeple."

For the next half hour, McGroarty showed me the basics of the swing—bringing the club up to a horizontal position behind my head—the left arm straight and the right elbow close to the body—turning the hips and shifting the weight from one foot to the other—keeping the head still.

As he left, McGroarty gave me one last word. " Now ye stay here an' practice, an' kaep outta paeple's way. And mind ye—take care a th'divots."

"Yes, sir," I replied, idly wondering what divots were.

I hoisted the club head over my head and hammered it down at the golf ball. Missing the ball completely, the mashie head excavated a huge chunk of turf, which sailed high into the air, showering me with dirt. How could a stupid little white ball just sitting on the grass be so hard to hit? I could understand it if a pitcher was throwing it from the mound, but it was just sitting there smiling at me. Actually, all of the golf balls McGroarty left were smiling at me, since they were well-used, driving-range balls, liberally laced with cuts in their covers resembling smiles. This ball had a smug grin like Stan Laurel. On the next swing, I finally hit it with the toe of the club head. Laurel merrily skipped off into the woods, no doubt in search of Hardy.

By mid morning, I had performed major surgery on the meadow grass with the mashie, lost five balls, and raised a healthy crop of blisters

*Missing the ball completely, the mashie head excavated
a huge chunk of turf.*

on the palm of my left hand. I heard the 'skritch-skritch' of McGroarty's knicker legs rubbing together as he came down the trail from the pro shop.

"I TOL' YE T'TAKE CARE O' THA DIVOTS!"

Frantically, I looked around in the surrounding trees, hoping to spot a divot and knock it silly with the mashie.

"Ye know wha' a divot is?"

"Uh...I guess not..."

"Ye don'a *guess* when ye talk t'me, ye *know* or ye *don' know.*"

I stood up straight. "I don't know what a divot is, sir."

McGroarty snatched a piece of loose turf from the ground and shoved it in my face. A piece of an earthworm, which had the bad luck to be living where my mashie had hit, hung out of the turf.

"*This* is a divot, ye blockhead. If ye were a member a th'club, ye'd hae' a caddy put it back in tha spot weer it came from, but since yurr only a member a th'proletariat, ye put it back yurrself." He put the divot into one of the many divot holes I had dug with the mashie and pressed it down with his shoe.

Glancing up the path toward the pro shop, McGroarty reached into one of the deep pockets of his knickers and drew out a well-worn silver flask. He unscrewed the top and took a lusty swig. Puckering up his massive eyebrows and squinching his eyes tight, he let out a deep sigh. His voice toned down to a furry whisper. "OK lad, now show me yurr swing."

I took a savage cut at one of the balls, clipping it on top and sending it rolling about six feet.

The tranquilizing effect of whatever McGroarty had in that flask evaporated when he saw my swing. "IF YE KAEP LOOKIN' OOP T'SEE WHERE TH'BALL'S GOIN' T'GO, YE WON'T'VE FAR T'LOOK...KAEP YER HEAD DOON!"

Vigorously, he hammered home some of the other basic instructions he had given me and left me with one final warning. "I see soome a th'balls I left here've escaped yurr charge. Ye better hope that they decide t'return before dark. God doesn't rain them t'me out'a th'heavens like manna, ye know."

The weeks drifted by into summer. School let out in mid June, a huge relief since I had been forced to relinquish the right-field job to a dumb girl, after I had compiled a school softball record of sixteen straight strike-outs. Figuring that my future in sports didn't lie with games where the ball moved *before* I hit it, my life became totally dedicated to golf.

Every morning after breakfast, I took the mashie out to the little clearing in the woods behind the pro shop and hacked away at the driving-range balls until dark. At first, half my time was spent looking for balls I had blasted into the surrounding trees, but my accuracy gradually got better. McGroarty would stop by three or four times a day, fortifying himself against his more affluent students by taking a nip or two from the flask and pointing out what I was currently doing wrong. His disposition didn't improve, but he must have been impressed with my practicing twelve hours a day, because he wasn't yelling at me as much as before.

I picked up golf terminology. The flat piece of ground where you took the first shot on each hole was the tee. But the little piece of wood that you stuck in the tee and put the ball on to take that first shot was *also* a tee. When the ball curved to the right, it was a slice—to the left was a hook. The big patches of sand scattered around the course were traps or bunkers. Knocking the ball out of a trap was blasting. The short grass surrounding the flag stick was the green. Rolling the ball into the hole that the flag stick was placed in was putting.

I soaked everything up like a sponge. The blisters on my left palm became thick, horn-like calluses, and my arms and face turned the same color as the head of my rust-pitted mashie, from many hours in the sun. On rainy days I prowled the pro shop, getting instruction from Jimmy, McGroarty's shop man, on replacing club grips, refinishing woods, or reweighting the head of a driver.

By late June, my mashie shots were consistently flying over one hundred yards, almost the length of the meadow. One afternoon when McGroarty stopped by, I felt I had to break the news.

"I'm done with the mashie, sir."

"What are ye talkin' aboot?"

"I'm hittin' the ball as hard as possible with this club—to the end of the meadow. I need t'practice with another club."

"Are ye sayin' ye've mastered th'mashie?"

"Yes, sir," I said proudly.

"I'll be sure t'drop a line t'tha professional at St. Andrews in Scotland. He may wish t'hire ye as a mashie consooltant." McGroarty grabbed my mashie, and bending over because of the shortness of the club, took a shot with one of my balls. It screamed out over the meadow, still climbing as it passed over the trees on the far end. He handed the club back to me. "While yurr lookin' furr that ball, ye'll hae time t'reflect on th'accuracy a yurr remarks."

But McGroarty must have admitted to himself that my lessons needed a new direction, because the next evening he took me out to the practice sand trap at the driving range.

The trap, like the ones on the course, was a huge yawning affair with a front end consisting of a vertical wall of sand terminating with an overhanging lip towering well over my head.

McGroarty threw a ball in the sand and stepped up to it. "Now, if ye try t'pick th'ball neat off th'sand, the front end a th'trap'll spit it back at ye. Ye mus' explode th'ball out." With that, he swung down with my mashie, hitting the sand with full force, well behind the ball. Through the cloudburst of sand, the ball popped out over the lip of the trap.

For two hours every evening I worked on trap shots with McGroarty's "exploding" technique. I had sand in my hair, ears, and eyes. I even had sand in my underwear. My breakfast eggs tasted gritty from the sand in my teeth. After a week, I finally quit trap shots when my mother gave me an ultimatum. Take a shower every night to keep the sand out of the bed or sleep in the sand trap.

But my appetite for expanding my golf skills had been whetted, and one evening I casually asked McGroarty if I could use the practice putting green.

"Th'mashie isn't meant fer pooting."

"Sir, it ain't meant for blastin' outta sand traps, either, but y'taught me how to use it for *that*."

McGroarty thought about that for a moment. "OK, but if ye scar up that pootin' green wi' th'mashie, th'greenskeeper'll nail yurr hide t'tha cloobhouse wall!"

"I'll take real good care a th'pootin'—I mean putting green, sir."

Gleefully, I ran over to the putting green and started in. Putting with a five iron was a tricky proposition. The ball hopped off for the hole like a goosed frog when you hit it, but I worked on it every evening when the green was deserted. As the summer drifted into late July, I started to look longingly at the tee of the first hole.

"Mr. McGroarty...it's six o'clock, and all the members are off the course. Kin I play the first hole?"

McGroarty was sitting at the cash register in the pro shop, counting the day's receipts. The glazed look in his eyes told me that he had hit the flask pretty hard and was in one of his mellower moods. The usual rock-set of his mouth had melted. I could even see his lips. If I was ever going to get on the course, this was the time. I held my breath.

He looked at me over his reading glasses. "Th'first hole? And have some cloob member see ye from th'window a th'Men's Grill? I think not."

Disappointed, I turned to leave.

"But if ye were t'go oot t'the seventeenth, oot a sight from the cloob-house, I'd say it'd be a wiser choice. But mind yurr divots oot there!"

Bounding out of the pro shop, clutching my mashie, I fished out a prime-condition driving-range ball from my pocket. I ran through the grove of trees lining the eighteenth fairway and in a few minutes was at the tee of the seventeenth hole. I put the ball down between the white tee markers and looked down the fairway.

The seventeenth hole was a wicked humdinger: a two-hundred-and-twenty-yard-par-three and the number-one-handicap hole, meaning that it was the hardest hole to par on the whole course. It was pretty to look at but had an ugly, unmerciful personality, being completely surrounded by trees planted in deep, six-inch-high rough. An elevated green sloping to the back was ringed by monstrous sand traps. To get the ball from the tee to the green required a long, accurate shot with enough backspin on the ball so it wouldn't roll off the back edge. It was not a nice hole.

But of course, I didn't know all that when I hit my first shot that evening—a beauty that soared off toward the flag—perfect direction and good distance. It hit the top of the ladies' tee and bounced forward into the tall grass just short of the fairway. At last—I was a golfer!

It was the best of all the summers I could remember. At five-thirty, I would gobble up my dinner in the employees' dining room and dash off to the seventeenth tee. I'd play the hole, pick up the ball, run the two hundred and twenty yards back to the tee with my mashie, and play it again. I could usually get in nine holes of golf—all at the same hole—before it was too dark to see the ball.

During the day I would still go to the meadow by the pro shop, now concentrating on the shorter pitch and chip shots. Experience playing the seventeenth hole had taught me that to improve my score I had to know how to get the ball close to the hole from just off the green. A long stick with a white handkerchief was my flag, and choking up on the grip of the mashie, I'd pitch the ball at the target from various distances. For shots that required even more accuracy, I would practice chipping the ball into an old wooden vegetable crate that I got from the clubhouse kitchen.

One morning in mid August, McGroarty came by the meadow just as I chipped two balls in succession into the crate from a distance of twelve feet. His eyebrows twitched involuntarily when the second one went in.

"S'tell me, lad, how many strokes are ye takin' t'get down on th'seventeenth hole, now?"

"Well, las' night I got real lucky an' gotta three, but mos' times it's fives or sixes. A coupl'a fours."

McGroarty's eyes narrowed. "Arre ye lyin' t'me?"

"No, sir! Why would I do that?"

"Ye holed out in three wi' th' wee mashie?"

"Yes, sir. It's the only club I got. But I'm still gettin' mostly fives an' sixes. I'm gonna do better before the summer's over."

"Ye know, there're full-grown men wi' a bagful a cloobs who've been playin' golf many more years than ye've been alive who've naer gotten three on that hole." That was as close as McGroarty had come to complimenting my golf game.

"Well...I been practicin' the hole a lot."

McGroarty took one last belt from the flask. "I'll tell Jimmy t'transfer my cloobs from th'leather bag into one a those canvas bags, so ye kin carry it. Tonight I'm goin' wi' ye."

"So now ye walk back t'the tee?"

"Well...I *run* back so I kin play the hole more times before dark."

We were standing on the seventeenth green that evening. McGroarty had just shot a solid par three, barely missing a birdie when he lipped a twenty-five-foot putt. I had pulled my approach shot into the sand trap in front of the green and gotten a five, but McGroarty didn't comment on my bad shot. Instead, he gave me tips on how to play the hole, pointing out that aiming my approach for the narrow apron to the green would reduce the chance of winding up in a sand trap.

We spent an hour on the green with McGroarty giving me an advanced course in putting. He threw several balls down at different places on the green so I could practice putting and memorize the curve, or break of the surface, from all angles. We got down on our knees, and he showed me how the direction that the blades of grass were pointing would affect the speed of the putt.

McGroarty pressed his finger into the green, explaining that the moisture in the sod was also a factor, and as I watched and listened, I realized what had taken place over the last three months. He had given me the mashie and basic golfing instructions back in early May just to keep me out of his way, but over time, McGroarty had begun to take a sincere interest in making me a good golfer. I had finally found a friend at Green Knolls.

But in late August, my blissful summer came to a sudden end. One afternoon at five-thirty, my mother, the old man, and I were sitting at a table in the employees' dining room. I was getting set to wolf down several breaded pork chops and run out to the seventeenth tee when the old man starting talking.

"I wuz jus' talkin' t'Smitty, the bartender in th'Men's Grill. Y'know, he always hears th'lowdown on everybody, an' he sez McGroarty's on his way out."

I slowly put down a pork chop. "What's that mean?"

"Well, the club has some kind'a Executive Council t'run things. They're havin' a meetin' th'Sunday before Labor Day, an' th'Council's gonna take a vote on whether or not t'keep McGroarty on as th'pro."

"But they'll vote t'keep 'im, won't they?" I said.

"Well, accordin' t'Smitty, this guy Brickhouse has talked enough people on th'Council into votin' against 'im t'swing th'vote."

"Who's Brickhouse?" I asked.

"Smitty sez he's th'head a th'Executive Council. Some high mucky-muck lawyer in Milwaukee."

My throat had tightened up, and I had lost my appetite completely. "But why would they wanna get rid of Mr. McGroarty?"

"I guess some a th'members don' like his cursin' on th'driving range. An' Smitty sez that Brickhouse, who's a real good golfer hisself, thinks that McGroarty's nuthin' but an over-tha-hill drunk. Smitty sez that McGroarty'll get a chance t'go t'tha Council meetin' an' say his piece, though."

I got up and ran out of the dining room.

"Hey," my mother said, "You didn't finish your pork chops."

"Mr. McGroarty, what would you do if you couldn't teach golf anymore?"

"Why do ye ask that, lad?"

I pitched another golf ball at the handkerchief flag at the far end of the meadow. "Oh...I dunno..."

McGroarty pulled the flask out of his knickers and unscrewed the cap. "I'd probably drink m'self t'death at a quicker pace than I'm doin' now." He took a nip and put it back in his pocket. In a quieter voice, he said "Been hearin' rumors in th'cloobhouse, hae ye?"

I couldn't look at him or speak. I just nodded. I waggled the mashie head behind the next ball, which seemed to be blurring. Suddenly his hand was on my shoulder, startling me since I had been staring at the ball. I looked at his ugly face, with its big red nose and fierce gray eyes. He had a trace of a smile. In all the months I had known him, I had never seen McGroarty smile. "Be of goud cheer, lad...they haen't got ould McGroarty oot th'door joost yet."

Since no one else came to the meadow at ten in the morning, when I heard footsteps on the path I expected to see McGroarty. It was Jimmy from the pro shop.

"McGroarty's goin' out fer a round a golf, an' wants you t'caddy fer 'im."

"Caddy? I ain't never been a caddy. I carried his clubs a couple a weeks ago, but I don't know nuthin' 'bout caddying."

"Look, all I know is McGroarty wants *you*. I put his clubs in the canvas bag again. It don't weigh much."

"But...my father sez ya haf'ta have a Social Security card t'caddy, an' I don' even know what that is. Even if I did, I'm not old enough to get one. He sez ya gotta be fourteen."

Well, that's prob'ly why McGroarty wants you, then. He won't have t'pay ya."

With McGroarty's clubs on my shoulder, I trudged up to the first tee, deep in thought. Why did he ask for me? Didn't he have enough problems without having me as a caddy? I was going to mess this up, I just knew it!

At the tee, another kid, quite a bit bigger than I was, stood ready with a huge leather golf bag. Pulling a toothpick out of the corner of his mouth, he looked me up and down. "Boy, Schultz is really hirin' 'em young these days."

"Who's Schultz?"

"You don't know the caddymaster's name? Where you been?"

"I'm not a regular caddy. I live here."

"G'wan...nobody *lives* at this place." He pointed at the canvas bag. "Whose bag izzat?"

"Mr. McGroarty's."

"Tha ol' buzzard hisself? Jeez! Oughta be a good round. I got Brickhouse. Caddied fer 'im before. Shoots about even par."

I pointed at the big leather bag. "Brickhouse? Why would McGroarty wanna play with Brickhouse?" This was *really* getting weird.

"Hey, do I look like I'm runnin' this place? How th'hell do I know? But ya know what Schultz tol' me when he called my number? Brickhouse usually plays with a guy named Donnelly, an' this mornin' they couldn't find Donnelly's clubs in the pro shop. How kin ya lose a member's clubs? Kin ya imagine how pissed off Donnelly must'a been when they call 'im up an' tell 'im they can't find his golf clubs?" What kind'a people does McGroarty hire at that pro shop, anyway?"

Before I could think of a reply, McGroarty and another man came out of the pro shop and walked up to us on the tee. Without saying a word, the man with McGroarty stuck out his right hand toward the other caddy and snapped his fingers. The caddy immediately pulled the driver out of the bag, jerked off the knitted head cover, and handed him the club.

Brickhouse was a tall, deeply-tanned, good-looking guy in his forties, wearing a light-blue sport shirt that I had seen for sale in the pro shop for twenty dollars. JWB was the monogram on the left breast pocket. Boy, I thought, if I had a shirt that cost twenty dollars, my mother wouldn't trust initials, she'd sew on my whole name.

Brickhouse clearly wasn't in a good mood. He wound up and snapped off a quick practice swing with the driver. The swing was professional-looking but vicious, the club head splitting the air so abruptly that I felt a gust of air like prop wash. "Do you think one of your boys stole Donnelly's clubs, Angus?"

McGroarty was surprisingly mild, almost good-natured. "Ach, na, Jack, probably someone jus' poot them in th'wrong bin. They'll turn oop this afternoon, count on it. Besides, it gae me an opportunity t'cancel lessons an' get in a round a golf wi' a furrst-rate player as yurrself. Th'least I kin do since Donnelly can't play."

Brickhouse took a cigarette out of a silver case and lit it with a matching lighter. "You're running a sloppy shop, Angus. Not watching those boys like you should."

I had been in the pro shop one night when a bag had been misplaced, and McGroarty had almost fired one of Jimmy's helpers. He ran the pro shop with an iron fist. He also never took the kind of insults that Brickhouse was dishing out. What was going on?

McGroarty and Brickhouse hit their drives, both booming shots down the middle of the fairway, but Brickhouse's was the longer by twenty yards. McGroarty took a six iron shot, hitting the fringe grass at the front of the green and bouncing the ball to within twenty feet of the pin.

Brickhouse took one last drag from his cigarette, flicked it on the fairway grass, pointed at it, and snapped his fingers. His caddy scooped up the butt, ground it out on the sole of his sneaker, and stuck it in his pocket. Brickhouse hit a solid seven iron, the ball hitting the green to the right of the flag and quickly coming to a stop with a small backspin bounce.

When we got to the green, the other caddy just stood there giving me a funny grin. "Well?"

"Well, what?" I said.

"McGroarty's ball wuz first on th'green. Yer supposed t'tend the flag."

"Tend the flag?"

"What's the trouble, here?" Brickhouse asked.

The other caddy now took great relish in exposing my ignorance. "This kid don' know how t'tend the flag. I dunno where he came from—I never seen 'im before, sir. I'll bet he's some caddy's younger brother, sneakin' up to the first tee t'try t'make some money on the sly. Sez he lives at the club. What a joke!" He shot me an evil grin.

Brickhouse gave McGroarty an aggravated look. "This is another example of what I'm talking about, Angus. Letting small kids sneak onto the course like this. No control! No wonder clubs are being stolen."

McGroarty spoke up, turning to the caddy. "What's yurr name?"

"Schmunk, sir."

"Well, Mr. Schmunk, it's true this yoong lad is not a regular caddy. However, he *does* live at th'cloob, and I've invited him along t'learn th'game. I would be vurry obliged if ye'll instruct 'im on th'proper procedures furr caddying furr th'rest a th'round. Ye kin start by showin' 'im how ye tend th'flag."

My heart slowly slid out of my throat and back down into my chest. Schmunk gave me a hateful look as he walked over to hold the flag stick while McGroarty and Brickhouse putted.

Both McGroarty and Brickhouse got their par fours on the first hole and matched each other, shot for shot, on the next two holes. The fourth hole was a four-hundred-and-ninety-yard-par-five. While Brickhouse was teeing up his ball, McGroarty starting talking to me in a raised voice. "Now, lad, this hole is where a yoonger, stronger man like Mr. Brickhouse has th'edge on me. Ye see those traps oot there aboot two hundred an' thirty yards? I mus' take great care not t'put my drive in them, while Mr. Brickhouse has th'ability t'drive way oer them, and have an iron shot left t'th'green furr a sure birdie, or possibly an eagle."

Brickhouse gave McGroarty a fleeting, insolent smile. "A good pro shouldn't have much trouble with those traps, Angus. They're really not that far out." He waggled the driver head behind the ball a few times and took his backswing.

McGroarty had always told me never to try for extra distance by taking a harder-than-usual swing, since that was a good way to come up with a slice. Being a scratch golfer, Brickhouse must have known this, too, but the thought of going up a stroke or two on McGroarty must have provoked him into thinking he could put an extra twenty or thirty yards on his drive with a little more mustard on the swing. On the backswing, he almost wrapped the driver around his body, then he slashed down on the ball, hitting it with whip-cracking ferocity.

The ball whistled off, a low line drive, streaking out toward the center of the fairway, but then it sliced, landing in the deep rough to the right.

"Gawdammit!" Brickhouse barked, dropping the driver at his feet.

McGroarty put a look of shock and dismay on his face, but somehow I knew he wasn't surprised at the slice. "Ach, whoot a pity, Jack."

Brickhouse stomped off the tee, leaving Schmunk to pick up the driver off the grass.

The deep grass in the rough gave Brickhouse enough problems to result in a bogey six, while McGroarty hit a nifty two iron shot to the green and two-putted for a birdie. After four holes, McGroarty was two up.

The fifth hole was a par four with two gigantic traps on the right side of the fairway halfway to the green. McGroarty's drive went right down the center of the fairway, and as he handed me his driver to put in the bag, he gave Brickhouse some fatherly advice. "Now, Jack, if yurr developin' a slice, ye want t'be vurry careful on this drive nae t'get th'ball in those sand traps.

I'd suggest rollin' yurr right hand over on th'downswing t'put a wee bit of a draw on th'shot. Nae too mooch, though. Joost a mite."

Why in the world did he say that? McGroarty told me *never* to think about my hands on the swing.

Brickhouse lit another cigarette, sucking most of it into ash on the first drag. "I am *not* developing a slice, McGroarty. Save your advice for the hackers, OK?"

But part of Brickhouse's brain must have subliminally processed McGroarty's words, because his drive had more than a "wee bit of a draw" on it. It was more like a full-fledged, screaming hook, still climbing as it passed over the deep rough on the left.

This time, Brickhouse didn't drop the driver, he reared back and threw it. Schmunk, who had been watching the flight of the ball, wisely decided he'd better watch the driver instead, which was now rivalling the ball for distance, sailing end over end into the rough. For a caddy to lose a member's ball was bad enough, but to lose a member's *club*, especially one that belonged to Brickhouse, could get Schmunk canned.

Schmunk found the driver but not the ball. With his lost-ball penalty stroke, Brickhouse wound up with a double-bogey six. McGroarty got a par, so after five holes, McGroarty was four strokes up.

Brickhouse's game didn't improve as the day wore on. He managed to sprinkle in a par here and there, but his drives were erratic, slicing or hooking into the unforgiving rough. When we got back to the clubhouse at the end of nine holes, Brickhouse sent Schmunk into the Men's Grill to get him a beer and a fresh pack of cigarettes to calm his nerves. On the back nine he chain-smoked, keeping Schmunk busy picking up the butts and putting them out on the sole of his shoe.

But nothing helped, and as we approached the seventeenth, the hole that had become a second home to me, Brickhouse was ten over par, down twelve strokes to McGroarty. For a guy with a one handicap, this was a very bad day.

McGroarty issued a sympathetic cluck every time a Brickhouse drive took off for the rough, but offered no more suggestions until we got on the seventeenth tee.

With a look of concern on his ugly face, McGroarty said, "Jack, knowing how yurr lookin' forward t'the Labor Day tournament, I might suggest a lesson or two wi'me t'straighten oot yurr long game. It would be a benefit t'ye, I'm sure."

Brickhouse's shaky composure snapped completely. His suntanned face became two shades darker, and there were flecks of saliva at the corners of his mouth. "McGroarty, the only thing I'm looking forward to is taking the Council vote next Sunday and getting your ass out of here."

McGroarty glanced briefly at Schmunk and me and then gave me a slow wink. "Indeed? Well, as loong as ye brought the subject oop in public, I hear that one of th'complaints is that I'm a wee bit harsh on soome people oot on th'practice tee."

"A wee bit harsh? You've really gotten a lot of members pissed off at you after you blasted them during a lesson."

"It's true. I have nae tolerance for rich people who think that payin' me ten dollars an hour will buy 'em instant skill. Golf is a undertaking that requires a vast amoont of patience and practice, and these people yurr referrin' to hae no inclination furr either. If they did, they'd be learnin', an' I would'nt be screechin' at 'em."

"*Nobody* can learn from a tyrant like you, McGroarty."

"Ye think nae? It so happens we hae here a perfect example a th'results a my severe teaching methods wi' a more receptive student." He pointed a finger at me.

I jumped like I had been stung by a bee.

McGroarty continued. "A few short months ago, this wee lad came t'Green Knolls, naer havin' laid eyes on a golf course in his life. I gae 'im one cloob an' put 'im t'work." He reached over, stuck his hand into his golf bag, and pulled out my mashie. "*This* cloob."

My gawd! What was my mashie doing in the bag? I had been carrying it around all day and hadn't realized it. How did it get there? I remembered putting it in the corner with the other old clubs when I went into the pro shop to pick up McGroarty's bag, but then Jimmy told me to go over to the display case and get three new balls for McGroarty's round. He must have snuck the mashie into the bag. What *was* going on? Whatever it was, I didn't like the direction it was taking.

Mcgroarty continued. "I moost confess, my initial motive was merely to kaep 'im from gettin' underfoot, but when I observed 'im practicin' from dawn t'dusk, th'possibility a 'im developin' into a fine golfer prompted me t'work wi' 'im further."

Brickhouse took the last cigarette out of a pack of Camels, crumpled up the empty pack, and threw it on the grass. He snapped his fingers and pointed at it. Schmunk scooped it up.

"That's all well and good, McGroarty, you working with the kid and all, but we're talking about *real* golfers here."

"Real golfers, indeed. If ye gi 'im one stroke on this hole, t'accommodate his wee size, this lad'll tie ye, or perhaps beat ye..." McGroarty held up my mashie. "Wi' this one club."

Omygawd! McGroarty had finally pickled his brain with the booze! If he wasn't careful, Brickhouse might take him up on it, and then where would I be? Even Schmunk, who had been pretty quiet since the first hole, got a chuckle out of it.

Brickhouse lit up his cigarette and snorted. "C'mon, let's quit fooling around here and play these last two holes. I need a drink."

"I am nae making a joke, Mr. Brickhouse. In fact, I'll pose a proposition t'ye. Gie th'lad a stroke on this hole, an' if ye beat 'im, I'll abide by th'Executive Council's decision wi' oot even attendin' th'meetin' in my oown defense."

It got deathly quiet on the tee. I developed a tic under my left eye. Brickhouse took a deep drag from his Camel and gazed at McGroarty for several seconds. "You're serious, aren't you?"

"Deadly serious."

"And he's going to play every shot with that little wooden club?"

"Every shot. He'll poot it in th'hole wi' th'mashie."

"One stroke? And if I win, you won't show up at the Council meeting to raise hell?"

"Coorrect."

"OK. Let's do it."

Schmunk and I had been sitting on the bench while all this was taking place. McGroarty came over and handed the mashie and his golf ball to me. "Ye have th'honors, lad."

"Mr. McGroarty, I can't do this..."

McGroarty dropped his voice a notch. "How many times ye played this hole?"

"Oh...couple a hundred, I guess..."

"Then ye *oown* th'hole. Play it once more—furr me."

My heart hammered under my ribs as I put McGroarty's new Spaulding Dot golf ball on the tee. The new ball radiated its whiteness like a spherical, fluorescent bulb. I had never hit a new ball before, and it heightened my anxiety. Then I remembered—I dug into my pocket and pulled out the driving-range ball I always carried around to use on this hole in the evening. I put it down on the grass and gave McGroarty his new Spaulding back. He smiled understandingly.

My tee shot went about one hundred and ten yards, landing on the near part of the small patch of fairway, about halfway to the green. Brickhouse took a last drag from the Camel, snatched a two iron from his bag and hit his shot. But like many of his drives that day, the shot sliced into the right-hand trap that guarded the green. Without a word, he dropped the club on the grass and stalked off toward the hole.

My stomach churned as I lined up the one-hundred-and-ten-yard second shot, but I looked at the flag and mentally transformed it into a white handkerchief on a long, straight branch, sitting in the far edge of the meadow. The shot hit the front edge of the green and trickled to within twenty feet of the pin.

Brickhouse had been standing on the edge of the sand trap where his ball was lying, and when he saw my second shot he twitched like he had been hit by a poison dart. Schmunk was in the process of pulling the sand wedge from the bag when Brickhouse grabbed the club so violently that he pulled the golf bag from Schmunk's grasp and it fell to the grass with a clatter of clubs.

My lie after only two strokes clearly unnerved Brickhouse. He didn't take enough sand on the trap shot, and the ball flew over the green, landing in another trap on the other side. Brickhouse wound up with a double-bogey five, and I putted out for a four. I didn't need the handicap stroke.

"I see it all now, McGroarty," Brickhouse barked, as he slung the putter off on the fringe of the green. "You set this whole thing up right from the beginning, didn't you? 'Losing' Donnelly's clubs to get on the course with me—destroying my game with your clever remarks—then bringing in this...this little *ringer* to make me look worse, so you can gloat about it at the Council meeting next Sunday."

McGroarty indulged in a slight smile. "I moost admit, it'll make furr a good, light-hearted story, to set th'tone furr my defense."

Brickhouse decided not to play the eighteenth hole after all. He stomped off towards the clubhouse, Schmunk trotting along behind with his clubs.

"What's a ringer? I asked McGroarty.

"A ringer? Ye might say it's someone who's a mite better than appearances let oon." He looked at me standing there in my bib overalls, white T-shirt, and old tennis shoes. "An' that's one a th'few things that Mr. Brickhouse got right today. Indeed, you doon't *look* mooch like a golfer."

"Well, McGroarty's one lucky Scotsman," the old man said as he gnawed on a pork chop bone.

I was sitting across the table from him in the employees' dining room. "Whaddaya mean?" I asked.

"Talked to Smitty this mornin'. He wuz tendin' bar at th'Executive Council meetin' yesterday. Said that Brickhouse passed around sheets with the meetin' agenda, an' McGroarty's name wasn't even on it. Somebody asked 'im about it, an' Brickhouse said he wanted to give McGroarty another chance, at least fer a year. It's hard to figure out them rich people."

I picked up my empty plate and looked at my mother. "Do ya think the cook'll give me a second helping on the pork chops?"

"Whaddaya mean gone?"

"He's gone," Jimmy said. "Left on the train fer Chicago last night and then on to New York. He sails for Scotland the day after tomorrow."

"But why didn't he tell me?" I asked.

"Didn't tell nobody, 'cept the club manager an' me. Had it planned for some time though. Got his tickets a couple a weeks ago. Asked me to give you these." Jimmy handed me a set of golf clubs in a canvas bag.

They weren't new but in excellent condition—a set of woods and irons, a sand blaster and a putter—longer than the mashie, but still shorter than standard.

"They got metal shafts," I said, fingering the clubs.

Jimmy smiled. "I know. I was the one who cut 'em to size. Worked lots a nights on those clubs."

"Thanks," I said quietly.

"He also asked me to give you this." He handed me a letter.
I opened it up.

To the Ringer:

I'm sorry for leaving so suddenly, but I am a poor man at saying farewell to good friends. Not enough good friends to practice on, I suppose.

First, forgive me for putting you in such a tight spot last week. Mr. Brickhouse was absolutely right. I set the whole thing up, and it was a selfish deed. I had two choices: throw myself on the mercy of the Executive Council, which I am too proud and bull-headed to do, or embarrass Brickhouse in such a way that he would drop the whole issue. As you no doubt have been told by Jimmy, I had planned my departure for some time, but I wanted it to be on my terms. You have made that possible.

I am sad to say that I will not be seeing you again. It is the persuasion of a doctor in Milwaukee that unless I stop drinking immediately, I'll not make it through the next year. I intend to get a second opinion on that since I cannot imagine any self-respecting doctor in Edinburgh telling a man such a foolish thing.

Nevertheless, professional golf is not a career for a person of my years, and I wish to spend the remainder of my time in the land where the sport first came into being.

Please accept the clubs with my good wishes. They're cut longer than the mashie, but next year you'll be that much taller.

Good fortune to you, my friend, and keep your head down.

Sincerely,
Angus P. McGroarty

I folded up the letter and put the bag of clubs on my shoulder. Blinking my eyes rapidly to clear my vision, I went to the front door, picked up the mashie where I had left it leaning against the wall, and brought it over to the cash register.

"Jimmy, how much do you want for this one?"

Home-Court Advantage

*Think the ball...into the basket...mind over matter...with
enough will power...and concentration...the body will
do...exactly what the brain commands...*

S tepping up to the free throw line, I spread my feet about three feet apart, carefully placing the toes of both tennis shoes right behind the line. Dribbling the ball a few times, I stared intently at the rim of the basket. I exhaled, and my breath condensed in the frigid gymnasium atmosphere, momentarily obscuring the rim. Grabbing the basketball with both hands and bending my knees slightly, I swung the ball between my legs and threw it underhanded up towards the basket—the accepted procedure for free-throw shooting at the time.

The shot was way short—the ball not even brushing the net. So much for mind over matter. Apparently my brain and body weren't on speaking terms this morning. It was going to be very tough making the varsity if I couldn't even hit the rim on free throws.

A gaggle of us B-Squad players were getting in some practice in the high school gymnasium on a chilly Saturday morning in mid February 1948. We had found out that the coach was going to be there to assess the recent water damage, and we still harbored the remote hope that a few spectacular shots would impress him sufficiently to consider us for the Iron Miners varsity team next year. When you were on the B-Squad in a high school with a total population of one hundred and twenty-nine, it didn't speak well for your stature in the sport of basketball, and you had to seize every opportunity to display your skill.

Paul O'Neal, our basketball coach, stared at my shot in utter disbelief but being the diplomatic sort, recovered and flashed me a thin, watery smile which I frantically accepted as encouragement. In his thirties with a tall, willowy build, he wore thick, horn-rimmed glasses and was considered more of a scholar than an athlete. Paul had been hired as the high school chemistry and physics teacher but made the mistake of letting it slip that he had played undergraduate basketball at Michigan Tech. Our tight-fisted school board seized this opportunity and twisted his arm into taking the coaching job on a part-time basis.

However, it turned out that O'Neal was a natural-born strategist of the game. For the first time that I could remember, our team had a chance to win more games than we had lost—to be decided by our final game this Friday. This had revived enough local interest in the sport to pack the gymnasium to capacity at every home game—three hundred and twenty-five people, including standing room by the popcorn machine.

Paul turned his attention back to Arvi Swanson, our local carpenter and handyman, to address the urgent business at hand. Arvi stood on the sideline and wagged his head slowly from side to side as he looked up at the gymnasium ceiling. "We're gonna haf'ta replace th'whole damned roof, but she can't be done till April or May when th'snow's gone. Till then, all I kin do is getta scaffold in here an' build a truss out'a two-by-eight lumber across th'width a th'ceiling to keep 'er from comin' down altogether."

The gymnasium ceiling looked like the soiled shirt front of a fat man whose belly had burst a few of the buttons. It had a precarious-looking bulge hanging down right over center court with dark moisture stains around the open crack where the melted snow had seeped through. The temperature, usually consistently low in Michigan's Upper Peninsula at that time of year, had lately bounced around like a yo-yo. A few days earlier, it had gotten up into the fifties and melted much of the thick layer of snow on top of the flat roof. The water collected at the center of the roof and proved to be too much for the aging structure. A gigantic leak resulted in a cascade of water onto the basketball court.

Then, to prove the adage that bad luck comes in streaks, the boiler used to heat the gym gave up the ghost at the same time that the temperature plummeted back down in the teens. While most of the water had been mopped up by then, the freeze had expanded the moist floorboards and buckled them badly. Large bumps and cracked boards were all over the whole basketball court surface—the wooden floor looked like Lake Superior on a choppy day.

Paul chewed absently on the end of a wooden pencil. "How about the floor? Is there anything that you can do about that?"

Arvi shook his head. "Ain't no sense fixin' th'floor till th'roof's replaced. You get another leak an' the floorboards'll buckle again."

"Well, can you fix the boiler so we can get some heat in here? We've got a game with St. Olaf on Friday."

"Not if I'm gonna truss up that roof. That'll take me all week."

"It's gonna be colder'n hell in here by Friday."

Arvi ambled toward the door. "Get somebody t'dye ten sets a long underwear with the school colors. That ought'a be a classy addition t'yer uniforms."

The following Monday morning I was sitting in the high school study hall, laboriously conjugating Spanish verbs, an academic pursuit of questionable value since any Spanish speakers were at least a thousand miles south of Upper Michigan. I got a tap on the shoulder. Paul O'Neal silently jerked his head, indicating that he wanted to talk to me out in the hall. As I followed him out, he also gathered up Reino Rovaniemi and Carl Kettu, two other B-Squad serfs. What was this all about? Ohmygawd! We were being cut from the B-Squad! The final indignity!

Out in the hallway, Paul pushed his horn-rimmed glasses up the bridge of his nose and spoke to the three of us in a quiet and serious tone.

"Clarence Hooker just told me that he's suspended three basketball players from playing in Friday's game because he saw them smoking in the bowling alley on Saturday night."

Clarence Hooker, the high school principal, had a long list of rules to live by for students in his charge. High on the list was no smoking. If Hooker caught you smoking on the school grounds, the chances were good that you'd find it much more difficult to puff on a cigarette with the fat lip he gave you. For basketball players the no-smoking rule applied whether or not you were on the school grounds.

"Who're the players?" I asked.

"Niemi, Sullivan, and La Beau."

One starting guard and both starting forwards! Without them, we were going to get slaughtered on Friday night against St. Olaf!

O'Neal continued. "Effective immediately, I'm putting the three of you on the varsity to come up with a full team of ten players. The chances are you won't get in the game, but don't be late for practice this afternoon." He walked off down the hallway.

Leaning up against the wall, I nonchalantly crossed my legs to keep from wetting my pants from pure ecstasy. The varsity! *I was on the varsity!* We were going to get our asses whipped on Friday, but one of those asses was going to be *mine!* A uniform with a real number on it! The bell rang, and I floated down to Spanish class on cloud nine.

It was a raggedy-looking crew that gathered around the coach in the middle of the frigid gymnasium at four-thirty. Although we had suited up for practice, almost everybody had on sweaters, and Reino Rovaniemi was wearing his plaid winter cap. O'Neal dribbled a basketball absently while he talked to us.

"We're adopting a new strategy on both offense and defense to deal with the loss of three of the starting five..."

Carl Petersen, our starting center and the tallest kid on the team at six foot one, irritably interrupted. "Coach, it ain't gonna make any difference what we come up with. Without Sullivan, La Beau and Niemi, St. Olaf's gonna roll right over us. Lookit this bunch! I'm the only guy left that's over six foot! An' gawd help us if we have to put any of these B-Squaders in the game!" He pointed a finger at me. "Have you ever watched *him* try to shoot baskets? St. Olaf's already beat us once this season, and that was when we had all of the starting five."

"Yes, but that was on their home court. This time they have to play on *our* court."

"*Our* court? We ain't even gotta court! Lookit this place! It's freezin' in here, the floor's all buckled t'hell, an' Arvi Swanson's puttin' up a truss the size of a railroad trestle across the ceiling to keep the roof from cavin' in. You won' even be able t'throw a decent pass in here when he's done."

O'Neal put the basketball on the floor and took out his wooden pencil that he chewed on when he was thinking. "Oh...I dunno...don't be so quick to give up. Keep in mind that *we* know what kind of shape this place is in, but St. Olaf doesn't." He gazed around the gym, and a trace of a smile started to play with the corners of his mouth. "Yes...the more I think about it, I'd say we have a definite home-court advantage."

The rest of the practice was taken up with dribbling the ball up and down the length of the court. Normally, nothing as basic as dribbling would be worked on this late in the season, but now there was nothing basic about dribbling a basketball in our gym. While a bounced basketball would normally come back to your hand like an obedient dog, the buckled floorboards gave the ball a deranged personality, rebounding it at totally unpredictable angles. After two hours we finally found paths where the floor was relatively flat, so we could dribble the ball from one end of the court to the other. It was like plotting a course through a mine field.

Since no hot water meant that taking a shower after practice was out of the question, we towelled ourselves off in the locker room and got dressed. O'Neal was waiting by the door when I left the gym and fell in step beside me.

"You know that you'll probably spend the game on the bench...but there's a special assignment I'd like you to take care of for me."

"Sure, Coach. Whaddaya need?"

"Well, the way I figure, it would be good if we could get some extra effort from the cheerleaders..."

The cheerleaders! This sounded like a very good assignment! "We got some pretty good cheerleaders, Coach...I think they'll get the crowd going pretty good, but ya want me t'hold some special meetings with 'em t'get 'em, like, motivated?" My pulse cranked up a couple of notches just at the thought.

"I was thinking that Barbara Bandini would make a good addition to the cheerleading squad."

"Barbara Bandini? Bowwow Bandini? Coach...you gotta be kiddin!"

Barbara Bandini, a.k.a. Bowwow Bandini, was nowhere on the list of girls that I would have considered as cheerleading material. Cheerleaders were slim-waisted and shapely-legged, with little, turned-up noses and fluffy personalities. Bowwow was cut from entirely different cloth. She had earned her nickname in the third grade when she bit off Toivo Kangas' earlobe during a heated dispute over a hopscotch game, and her disposition had gone downhill ever since. Now, at seventeen and a half, she was five foot eleven and weighed in at about one hundred and ninety pounds. She had dark, greasy hair tied up in a bun, a wispy mustache that I would have been proud to own, and more hair on her legs than I had on my head. Bowwow lived on a farm out in the Dead Dog River location and only came in to town to go to school. The older kids used to call her by her nickname until she closed in on her true fighting weight and dealt out a few well-placed left jabs.

O'Neal took out his wooden pencil and began to nibble on it. "You gotta admit though, she really knows how to yell."

He had that right. Bowwow's only concession to socializing was hog-calling contests. Last fall, she had won first prize at the Marquette County Fair. For sheer volume and vocal range, Bowwow was major-league. Her "SOOUUEEEEEEEEEEEEEE" started out at a modest sixty decibels but built up to a skull-cracking crescendo at the C above the C above high C. Dogs whimpered and ran into the woods—window panes rattled—huge icicles dropped off the eaves. Old man Mattila claimed that he was driving by the Bandini farm one day when Bowwow was calling in the pigs, and she cracked the windshield on his '37 Ford.

O'Neal continued. "The way I figure it, if Bowwo...uh...Barbara was to give a team cheer, especially when the other team had the ball, it might prove to be disconcerting to the opposition—know what I mean? Another little added home-court advantage, so to speak."

Disconcerting to the opposition! How about the rest of us? As far as I knew, Bowwow had never cut loose indoors before. Could the roof take the strain?

"So how do I figure into this, Coach?"

"As a faculty member, it's not my place to get involved, so I want you to ask her to do it."

The next morning Rovaniemi and I stood by the main entrance as the school bus unloaded its passengers. I had recruited Reino to take part in the operation just in case Bowwow became violent and I needed someone to pull her off of me. Bowwow trudged up the icy sidewalk, idly picking her nose. I stepped out in front of her.

"Good morning, uh...Barbara. Gotta minute?"

"Whadda you two turds want?"

"Ya know, we got our final basketball game with St. Olaf on Friday?"

"So?"

"Well, the coach figures that...if we can really get the crowd behind us...we might stand a chance of winning the game...even though we're missing three of the regular players."

"Git outta my way."

"Uh...Coach wanted me to ask ya if you'd join the cheerleader squad for the final game."

I had used enough sense to stay out of reach, but Reino had wandered a little too close. Bowwow's right arm shot out; she grabbed the front of his mackinaw, reeling him in like a frog snapping a fly, until their noses were about two inches apart. Her close-set, flinty gray eyes bored holes into Reino's head, and her mustache twitched as she hissed into his face.

"It really pisses me off when people make fun a me."

Reino squealed in terror. "Lemme go! It wasn't my idea—I jus' came along to be his bodyguard!"

I jumped in. "It's no joke, Barbara. The coach sez that with your mouth...uh...vocal ability, you could really make a difference in the game." Then a true inspiration struck me. "An' we'd like t'have ya do some a your famous hog calls during halftime."

Her grip on Reino loosened up a fraction, and I knew I had struck a chord. "What time's the game?"

"Eight o'clock Friday night. But you ought'a see the coach today about practice."

"Practice? I don' need no practice yellin'." With a flick of her right wrist, she sent Reino tumbling into a grimy snowbank next to the sidewalk and resumed her march to the front door.

"Well, they might want to take your...uh...measurements for...uh...cheerleader's uniform."

Bowwow turned around and gave me a brutal sneer. "A uniform? Yer pissin' me off again!"

For the next three days, practice sessions were taken up with Coach O'Neal's new offensive and defensive strategies. Instead of our usual zone defense, we adopted a man-to-man defense so that if their players lost the ball dribbling on the uneven floorboards, we would be right there to scoop it up.

Our most serious problem was now we had only one guy, Petersen, the center, who could score baskets with any kind of consistency. So O'Neal had him working feverishly on hook shots from every spot around the basket. The main job of the other four guys was to get the ball to Petersen.

After practice on Thursday night, Carl Kettu and I left the gym together. Carl was dribbling a basketball all the way home, figuring it was good practice since the ice and snow on the road combined with the gravel that the Township threw on it constituted a reasonable facsimile of our gymnasium floor. "You really talked Bowwow into joining the cheerleader squad?" Carl asked.

"I wouldn't say that she actually joined the squad. She didn't break any of our bones, and she asked what time the game started. I figure she'll show up. Too bad she's not a guy...we could use some'a her muscle under the backboards to pull in rebounds."

Carl had a conniving smile on his face. "I been thinkin' 'bout another idea fer improvin' our home-court advantage tomorrow night, an' you an' me could pull it off..."

"If it's anything like the Bowwow Bandini assignment, I don' wanna hear it."

"Lissen...we drive out to After-Shave's camp tomorrow afternoon an' bring him into town. He'll get slopped up at the Jack Pine Bar, an' maybe he'll find his way to the game again, like he did last month."

I stopped dead in my tracks. "That's the worst idea I ever heard in my life! If Hooker found out we done sumthin' like that, we'd get expelled.

Besides, it's only the middle of the month, an' After-Shave ain't been paid yet."

"Bruno at the Jack Pine is nuts about basketball. He'd let After-Shave drink on credit if he thought that After-Shave would start sumthin' crazy up at the gym again an' help the team get loose."

After-Shave was a pulp cutter who lived out in the bush and only got into town at the end of each month, wages in hand, with the sole purpose of drinking up all of the booze at the Jack Pine Bar. He got his nickname one Sunday morning when he broke the front window of Nardi's Drugs and Notions and helped himself to some bottles of Aqua Velva after-shave on display. The Aqua Velva was for medicinal purposes only, of course—being useful to ward off the charging herd of pink elephants that frequently sought out After-Shave on Sunday mornings before the bars opened. And he definitely had been getting the upper hand on the elephant problem—dropping three or four of the pesky critters with every swallow—until old man Nardi came up behind him and gave him the ultimate tranquilizer with the business end of a pipe wrench.

But the incident that inspired Carl's hair-brained idea had occurred on the last Friday in January when, after putting a sizable dent in the Jack Pine's liquor supply, After-Shave lurched into the gymnasium where the Iron Miners were being humiliated by the Michigamme Badgers. At first he just stood at the sideline, weaving gently with the ebb and flow of the game, thoroughly enjoying himself, although he didn't know a jump ball from a jockstrap. All that elbow bending at the Jack Pine Bar must have tired him out, because suddenly he decided to take a nap and fell face down on the floor. Unfortunately, his head was on a collision course with a Michigamme guard who was taking the ball down court—the guard, basketball, and After-Shave all went flying in three different directions.

The referee decided that some kind of foul had to be called, and furiously blowing his whistle, stood there pointing his finger at After-Shave. All this racket woke After-Shave, and he staggered to his feet. Being of a competitive nature, he figured he could blow that whistle at least as good as the referee, so he grabbed it from the referee's mouth and started to blow it himself. Since the whistle was attached to a short cord looped tightly around the referee's neck and the referee was a good ten inches shorter than After-Shave, he suddenly found himself being hoisted up the front of After-Shave's filthy plaid shirt.

After-Shave, looking down on a dark head of hair snuggled up on his chest, figured that someone had started up the music and a cute brunette in a striped blouse wanted to dance with him. So he put both arms around the referee's waist and started to waltz slowly around the gym floor, blowing the whistle in three-quarter time.

The crowd, of course, lapped this up and gave them both a standing ovation. All this uproar revitalized the Iron Miners, and they reeled off a flurry of baskets to pull out a victory.

However, Clarence Hooker didn't see any humor in it at all. He told the coach that whenever we had another home game that coincided with After-Shave's payday, he wanted guards at the gymnasium door.

Carl continued to unfold his plan. "I'll have the old man's pickup truck tomorrow. I figure that if we leave town about four-thirty, it'll be dark when we get back, an' nobody'll notice us bringin' him in."

I stared moodily out the windshield at the two ruts in the snow that passed for a logging road. It was a quarter to five on Friday, and the late-afternoon, pale winter sun was casting long shadows from the spruce trees. "What if he won't come t'town with us?"

Carl smirked from behind the wheel. "You kiddin'? With a chance to lap up booze on credit at the Jack Pine? He'll come." Carl reached underneath the seat and brought out a bottle of Fox Deluxe beer. "Besides, I lifted three a these from the case my old man has in the back porch to keep After-Shave occupied on the trip back to town."

"But they're not gonna let him in the gym."

"That's the beauty of the plan. Nobody's expectin' him to be in town. Hooker doesn't know, an' the boys down at the Jack Pine sure as hell ain't gonna say anything—they wanna see the fun. It'll only be ol' Wesley Sullivan collectin' tickets at the gym door, an' After-Shave outweighs him by 'bout one hunnert fifty pounds." Carl stared intently out of the windshield. "There's his camp up ahead."

After-Shave lived in a small, tar-paper-covered shack by the side of the logging road. Smoke curled up from a stovepipe jutting out of the roof. He was by the front door, chopping firewood with a double-edged ax. He stopped chopping, walked over to the passenger-side door, and leaned over to peer in at us.

It was hard to tell how old After-Shave was since his skin was weather-beaten to the extreme and every line in his face was permanently etched with dirt. There were rivulets of dried snuff juice that ran from both corners of his mouth to the jaw bone. His pale-blue eyes were terminally bloodshot and sunk into his head. He'd had six-days' growth of beard every time I had ever seen him, and today was no exception. It appeared that he cut his own hair about once a year—probably with the ax that he held in his hand. A huge guy—six foot five and two hundred seventy pounds—hands the size of my fielder's glove. He squinted, not recognizing either one of us.

"What day izzit?"

"Friday," I squeaked.

"I don't give a damn 'bout Friday or Saturday or Sunday! What day a the month izzit?"

"Uh...the fifteenth."

That was obviously not the answer he wanted to hear. "What th'hell you want, then?" He started to straighten up, slowly raising the head of the ax a couple of feet from the ground, as if he might chop a fender off the truck to vent his displeasure that it was only the middle of the month.

Carl leaned over me from behind the wheel and gave him a disarming smile. "We gotta big basketball game tonight, an' we figured you might wanna come into town an' see it."

"Ain't got no money. No sense goin' inta town without money."

"Bruno over at the Jack Pine Bar sez you can drink on credit an' settle up with him at the end a the month."

After-Shave stared at him for a full fifteen seconds. Then, he turned and with a quick overhead sweeping motion, buried the head of the ax deep into a nearby innocent birch tree. He opened the passenger-side door of the truck, and I quickly scooted over into the middle of the seat. He got in and slammed the door shut.

"If yer lyin' t'me, I'll cut yer nuts off."

With this added incentive to see his plan to successful completion, Carl quickly turned the truck around, and we headed back to town.

I had never been this close to After-Shave before, and he exuded a fragrance that fifteen bars of Lifebuoy wouldn't dent. The only thing that saved us was that he kept the truck window rolled down and the fresh, icy winter wind whistled into the cab.

Carl pulled out a bottle of Fox Deluxe from beneath the seat and handed it over to After-Shave. "I brought along some beer in case you wanted to relax a little on the way into town. There's a bottle opener in the glove compar..."

But After-Shave had already put the bottle to his mouth, wrenched off the cap with his molars, and downed three quarters of the contents before Carl could finish the sentence. He took a breath, finished the bottle, and flung it out into the snow. He put a giant paw across my chest for Carl to put another beer in it. Carl quickly reached down and gave him the second bottle.

He let out a magnificent belch that rattled the windshield. "Wut's this basketball yer talkin' about?"

Seeing that After-Shave was starting to get a little more receptive after the beer, Carl pressed forward. "Remember a coupla weeks ago when you were in town an' you went up to the gymnasium when we were playin' basketball?"

"Oh, yeh, I 'member some a that...they wuz throwin' this ball around."

"That's right...an' you were the star of the game."

"I wuz? I don' 'member that. Wha'd I do?"

"Well...you danced with a referee."

"I did? I don' 'member that. This referee...wuz she good lookin?...are referees them women in th'short dresses that holler a lot?" He finished the second beer and tossed the bottle out into the growing darkness.

Carl thought for a few seconds as he handed After-Shave the last Fox Deluxe. "That's right...you had a good-lookin' one...lots of dark, curly hair."

After-Shave grinned for the first time. He was missing three or four front teeth...no doubt a result of heated philosophical discussions in the Jack Pine Bar. "I would'n mind kissin' one a them referees...ain't kissed a woman yet."

"You mean...not ever?"

"Tha's right. I'm a virgin."

"A big strappin' guy like you...it's hard t'believe."

No, it's not, I thought.

Carl decided he'd better steer the conversation to the business of tonight's game. "We're playin' a tough team tonight...St. Olaf...they're a Catholic school in Marquette."

After-Shave scowled at the snow reflected in the headlights. "Cath'lics, huh? Ain't got much use for Cath'lics." He took a healthy swig, emptying the last beer.

Carl lowered his voice to a conspiratorial tone. "Not only that, it's a private school, an' you have to be pretty well off to get in there. They're rich Catholics."

"Rich Cath'lics! Be damned! Poor Cath'lics is bad enough! I'll kick th'ass off any rich Cath'lic I see!" And to punctuate his opinion, he smashed the empty bottle on the outside of the truck door and flung the jagged neck into the darkness.

Fortunately, we were just pulling into town, and a moment later Carl stopped the truck in front of the Jack Pine Bar. After-Shave got out and strode towards the bar.

Carl opened the driver's-side door and stood on the running board, yelling after him. "DON'T FORGET THE GAME AT EIGHT O'CLOCK! REMEMBER...WE'RE WEARIN' THE BLACK UNIFORMS! THE GOOD GUYS'RE DRESSED IN BLACK!"

After-Shave didn't even look back. He already had his mind on business in the Jack Pine as he jerked open the door to the bar.

I yanked the sleeve of Carl's mackinaw. "Carl, shaddup! You want the whole town to know we brought him in?"

Carl cackled with glee and put the truck in gear, the rear wheels throwing snow as we sped off toward the gym. I had an uneasy feeling in the pit of my stomach. We may have just let a great white shark loose in a water polo match.

At six-thirty we were already suited up and running through warm-up drills in the gym. O'Neal had, in part, taken Arvi Swanson's advice and procured ten sets of long underwear tops which we wore underneath the sleeveless uniform jerseys to combat the cold. Unfortunately, the underwear was red, clashing violently with the orange and black of the uniforms. We looked like Baltimore orioles with a skin disease.

But the adrenaline surging through my body had insulated my whole being from the adverse playing conditions. I looked down at my chest, admiring the stunning, orange "26" emblazoned on the black jersey, already scheming how I could talk the coach into letting me keep the uniform after the game for mounting on my bedroom wall. We were undoubtedly going to lose the game, but for me it was a magical night.

An icy blast of air whistled in from the door, and I turned to see the St. Olaf team trooping in. I was at the game that we lost to them on their home court in mid December. How could all ten of them have grown six inches in only two months? They walked in with a lithe, confident swagger, dressed in exquisite white and red jackets, gazing around the gym with amused smirks. Bringing up the rear was their coach, a short, swarthy man dressed in an expensive topcoat and clenching a long cigar between loose, rubbery lips. He bore an uncanny resemblance to Edward G. Robinson. Stopping in front of O'Neal, he took the cigar out of his mouth and looked around slowly.

"What was this place before they condemned it?" He knelt down and fingered the end of a floorboard sticking up a half an inch. "Wait a minute...don't tell me...I got it! You have horse races in here in the summertime! Plow horses, from the looks of this floor."

O'Neal gave him a polite smile. "Well, we've been having some problems with a leaky roof...we'll get the roof and floor replaced this spring."

"You better turn on the heat. The game starts at eight, don't it?"

"Well...see...we had this problem with the boiler, too."

"No heat?"

"No heat."

"Are we really going to play a basketball game in here tonight?"

O'Neal took out his pencil and started to chew on it. "Unless you want to forfeit."

"Forfeit? We'll whip your asses in the snow if we have to! Show me where the locker room is!"

By seven-thirty the gymnasium had started to take on an aura of excitement. The usual two rows of metal folding chairs that had been put out around the sidelines were filling up rapidly. People filed in carrying their popcorn and soda pop that they bought at the door. Since the soda pop had been stored in the cold gym all week, each bottle had a thick layer of icy slush in it. But it was the traditional drink at basketball games, and nobody seemed to mind. Not too many people took off their hats and coats, though. Nobody expected us to win the game, especially with three starters benched, but it was the last game of the year, and under Coach O'Neal's tutelage the team had done better than expected.

Bowwow Bandini showed up at quarter to eight, and O'Neal had a few words with her. She was dressed in bib overalls, sheepskin jacket, and a plaid woolen cap, so it didn't cross anybody's mind that she was in the cheerleading business.

The St. Olaf team was practicing at the opposite end of the court, and while their warm-up drills were majestic to watch, their longer shots weren't on target. During the week we had found out from experience that if you're shooting a basketball in near-freezing temperatures, your hands are too cold for good fingertip control. When they had first arrived, the St. Olaf players had pointed at the red underwear underneath our jerseys and snickered, but now I noticed that the pale-blue goose bumps on their arms didn't match their uniforms any too well, either.

The referee arrived, and I was relieved to see that he wasn't the same one After-Shave had picked as his waltzing partner. After the referee and the two coaches had an extended conversation about Arvi Swanson's overhead truss, they decided that any ball hitting the truss was still in play.

Minutes before the start of the game, O'Neal gathered us around him at the home bench for last-minute instructions. He started off by singling out the three newly promoted B-Squad players. "Now if by chance any of you three get into the game, remember that this isn't a shirts-and-skins game. Just because you've got a shirt on doesn't mean that everybody with a shirt is your teammate, so be careful who you pass the ball to."

My face burned. Gawd! What kind of dummies did he think we were? At the preliminary game that took place before the varsity event, custom dictated that the visitors took off their shirts while the home team got to wear theirs, since the lowly B-Squad teams didn't have uniforms.

Promptly at eight o'clock the referee blew his whistle and both starting fives took to the floor. The Iron Miners had Smoky La Farge, five-foot-ten, and Clyde Bertucci, five-foot-nine-and-a-half, as starting forwards; Carl Petersen, six-foot-one, at center; and Hake Hanson, five-foot-eleven, and

Mutt Hukala, five-foot-nine, at the guard positions. We were giving away at least two or three inches in height at every position to the St. Olaf team.

The crowd hushed as the centers crouched, and the referee held the ball between them with his open palm for the opening tip-off. He threw the ball high into the air.....................

The ball was still travelling upward at a good speed when it struck Arvi Swanson's ceiling truss and ricocheted toward the home basket. This took St. Olaf completely by surprise, and their center feebly swatted at the ball as it whizzed over his head. O'Neal had alerted us of this possibility, and our forwards had already broken down court toward our basket. La Farge fielded the ball and went in for an easy lay-up. The crowd whistled and cheered as we drew first blood, and the St. Olaf coach stood up with his mouth hanging open, the cigar falling to the floor. But there was nothing he could say. The decision had already been made—any ball hitting that truss was still in play.

The St. Olaf guards tried to take the ball down toward their basket but quickly discovered the ball had a mind of its own when dribbled on the lumpy floor. Bertucci picked up an errant dribble and drove in for another easy lay-up. Four to nothing. Finally, after some cautious passing, St. Olaf got the ball down in the area of their basket. One of their forwards neatly faked out Hake Hanson and had a clear set shot. He took careful aim...

Bowwow Bandini, sitting a few chairs down from our bench, jumped to her feet, and with the cords in her thick neck popping out, opened her mouth.

"DEEEEEEEEEEEEEEEEEEE......FENSE!!!!!!!!!!!!!!!!!!!!!"

Bowwow's yell sounded like a head-on collision of two ore trains. At least fifty people dropped their slushy soda pops on the floor. With their eyes popping out, our regular cheerleaders turned to look at Bowwow with shock and envy. The St. Olaf coach again dropped his now-mangled cigar on the floor. The shot their forward was making went clear over the backboard.

As soon as everyone recovered, a big cheer went up, and several people gave Bowwow a standing round of applause—somewhat muted since everybody was wearing mittens. Our cheerleaders got up and delivered their routine "ORANGE AND BLACK—FIGHT! FIGHT!" but it sounded puny by comparison, and no one paid them much mind. The crowd was waiting for

Bowwow's yell sounded like a head-on collision of two ore trains.

Bowwow's next sonic blast. Several guys put down the ear flaps on their wool caps in anticipation.

The rest of the first quarter was pretty much more of the same. Every time St. Olaf tried a set shot, Bowwow would jump up and let loose with "DEE-FENSE!" They were clearly rattled, and when the whistle blew signaling the end of the first quarter, the score was:

Iron Miners — twelve
St. Olaf — four

The St. Olaf coach stormed across the court to our bench, and pointing at Bowwow, he snarled at O'Neal, "Can't you shut up that...that gawddamned noise?"

O'Neal just calmly stared at him. "This is a basketball game, not a golf tournament. People yell at basketball games."

"That's not yelling! That screech owl is practicing psychological warfare!"

Bowwow bounded out of her chair, and grabbing the St. Olaf coach by the lapels of his expensive topcoat, she lifted him up on his tiptoes. "Whud'id you call me, you li'l fart?"

The crowd hushed suddenly to an expectant buzz. Getting to see Bowwow Bandini spill some enemy blood was an added attraction they hadn't counted on.

The snarl wilted on his face. "Hey, take it easy, buddy, I jus..." His eyes narrowed as he gave Bowwow a double take. "My gawd, you're a woman!"

I fully expected that those would be the last words he would utter. Bowwow let go of his coat with her right hand and was winding up with a rock-like fist to hammer him senseless, when O'Neal and Petersen jumped in and pried them apart.

A sigh of disappointment rippled through the crowd. The St. Olaf coach stomped back to his own bench as the referee blew the whistle signaling the beginning of the next quarter.

The second quarter was another low-scoring affair, but in the closing minutes of the first half of the game, one thing was becoming unpleasantly clear. St. Olaf was adapting to the adverse playing conditions. Their guards had found the paths along the court where you could dribble the ball without losing it, and our forwards were picking up fouls while trying to force the turnovers that had come so easily in the first quarter. Even though Bowwow jumped up and screamed "DEE-FENSE!" on their set shots, a few of those shots were good. At the end of the first half our lead had shrunk to three points.

The fact that we had any kind of lead at all had the home crowd in an expansive mood, and when Bowwow gave her famed hog calls as the major halftime event, she received an enthusiastic reception. However, some of the guys took the opportunity to observe a time-honored tradition—taking half-empty pop bottles out to their cars to stiffen up the drink with their own private stock.

Our worst fears were realized in the third quarter. St. Olaf had become acclimated to the gymnasium floor, the cold temperature, and hard as it was to believe, Bowwow's screams. They started to move the ball confidently up the court, scoring with consistency. To make matters worse, La Farge picked up his fifth foul late in the third quarter and had to leave the game. The bench strength was down to four—and three of us were B-Squaders. My pulse started to speed up. Making the varsity was all I had wanted, being perfectly happy to sit out the whole game on the bench. Gawd! What if I had to play?

The whistle blew ending the third quarter. The score:

St. Olaf — thirty-four
Iron Miners — thirty-one

As the fourth quarter rolled along, the mood of the crowd took on an air of quiet resignation—another loss and another losing season. While Petersen was doing his best, scoring hook shots, we were losing ground to St. Olaf. They now moved the ball effortlessly up the court, scoring at will and controlling rebounds with their height advantage. The St. Olaf coach had a relaxed, snotty-looking grin on his face as he puffed on a fresh cigar.

Bowwow jumped up on one of their now frequent set shots.

"DEEE.......FEuuurrrkkk." She grabbed her throat, coughing hoarsely.

I got up from the bench and went over to her. "Barbara—you OK?"

"They're takin' s'many shots that my throat's givin' out. That's it fer tonight. I can't yell no more."

Great! With Bowwow out of commission, we were totally doomed.

Suddenly, there were loud voices in the front entrance lobby. An explosion of breaking glass sounded like a case of soda pop had been thrown against the wall. Wesley Sullivan came scurrying into the gym from his ticket-taking post at the door. The inside door burst open, swinging over and hitting the wall with a splitting crash.

After-Shave had come to watch the basketball game.

He stood there in the doorway, listing about thirty degrees to starboard. To call After-Shave drunk would have maligned the very word. He was two light-years past drunk. The whites of his eyes had been completely transformed to blood red. A gigantic pinch of snuff hung half in and half out of the corner of his open mouth, quietly dripping juice from his whiskery jaw bone. His fly was open, and some of his dirty, red plaid shirt peeked out. The cheerleaders gasped and pointed, thinking no doubt, that they were witnessing the ravages of some exotic social disease.

But the most arresting feature of After-Shave's appearance was the long, nasty gash in his right cheek—the result of being on the losing end of a jousting match at the Jack Pine Bar involving broken beer bottles. Blood was flowing quite freely from the gash, collecting in a puddle on the floor.

He lurched forward like Frankstein's monster, clutching a paper bag with a bottle inside, dribbling blood across the gym floor. The game was halted while he staggered across the floor and veered over to the sideline by our bench. He spotted Mrs. Hoaglund, our Spanish teacher, and giving her a wide, snuffy grin, headed straight for her. She quickly hurried for the door. With a thundering crash After-Shave collapsed his big frame onto the chair she had just vacated. People on both sides of him also left. One thing you had to say about After-Shave—he got choice seating wherever he went.

During the lull in the action, the St. Olaf coach walked over to our bench and said to O'Neal, "That drunk—aren't you going to get him outta here—call an ambulance or something? Looks like he's hurt bad."

"Ambulance? We haven't got an ambulance in this town."

"Well, at least get him to a doctor."

"The closest doctor is in Michigamme—only comes here on Tuesdays." O'Neal jabbed a thumb at After-Shave. "Besides, he always winds up looking like that when he comes to town. I've seen him losing much more blood than that." Then O'Neal took out his pencil, nibbled on it, and put a concerned look on his face. He pointed to the large hunting knife stuck in the top of After-Shave's boot. "But you'd better tell your boys to stay away from him, though. He can be dangerous when he's had a few."

The game resumed, but somehow you could feel the momentum starting to shift. When one of the St. Olaf players lost his footing on After-Shave's blood on the floor, it was a portent of things to come.

Hake Hanson was bringing the ball down court when one of the St. Olaf forwards reached out and neatly stole the basketball. Chuckling triumphantly, he was dribbling down the sideline towards the St. Olaf basket for a sure two points, when he was abruptly jerked to a halt. After-Shave had reached out and grabbed him by the back of his trunks, pulling him out of bounds to have a little discussion about the morality of stealing basketballs.

"Don't do that no more," After-Shave whispered hoarsely. "Now, give it back!"

The petrified kid threw the ball back to Hanson as the referee came bouncing over, frantically blowing his whistle. The whole crowd held its collective breath. Was it going to be waltz time again?

But the referee marched over to O'Neal, pointing his finger at After-Shave. "Throw that bum outta here—he's interfering with play!"

O'Neal looked over at After-Shave who was now unconcernedly fortifying himself from the bottle in the paper bag. "You have any suggestions as to *how* we're gonna throw him out?"

The referee made a half-hearted threat of forfeiting the game to St. Olaf, but after noticing After Shave glaring at him with blood-red eyes, he meekly went back out on the court.

Seeing that After-Shave wasn't going to get thrown out galvanized the crowd. People stood up, yelling and whistling as the teams surged up and down the court. The Iron Miners had been down by nine points when After-Shave made his entrance, but now they picked up the frenzy from the crowd and started to close the gap. Mutt Hukala stole the ball twice and scored a couple of baskets—the deficit was quickly reduced to five points.

Bowwow got up, walked over to After-Shave, and said a couple of words. He gave her a bleary smile and handed over his paper bag with the bottle. Bowwow took a big mouthful and just stood there for several seconds, gargling vigorously. When she was done, she swallowed, handed him the bottle, and sat down.

Whatever was in the bottle must have agreed with Bowwow's throat because the next time St. Olaf was taking a shot, she jumped up.

"DEEEEEEEEEEEEEEEEE......FENSE!!!!!!!!!!!!!!!!!!!!!!!"

It was gratifying to see Bowwow back in form.

The shot bounced off the rim, and there was a mad scramble for the ball. In the scuffle the ball got kicked and skittered for the sideline. Since Bertucci was the last one to touch it, it was going to be St. Olaf's ball. The ball hit After-Shave's boot, and he reached down and picked it up—a St. Olaf player hurried over to the sideline to put it in play.

Seeing the enemy approaching, After-Shave concluded that the only thing to do was to shoot the ball at one of the five baskets he saw shimmering in the distance. He pressed the ball firmly between his giant paws for a long set shot.

POWWWWWWWW!!!!!!!!

The ball exploded in his hands, deflating to a limp, rubbery rag. Not knowing what else to do, After Shave handed the dead basketball to the St. Olaf player, clearly unnerving the kid to the extent that he just stood there open-mouthed until the referee gave him another basketball. The referee shot After-Shave a nasty glare, but how could you fault a guy for just squeezing a basketball a little too hard?

Just as we were closing the gap, another blow was dealt to the Iron Miners when Bertucci picked up his fifth foul and had to leave the game—the bench was now down to the three B-Squaders. The icy hand of fear clutched my heart.

Bowwow got up and hit After-Shave's bottle again, taking two large swallows. Apparently, she was getting caught up in the excitement of the game, because this time she forgot to gargle. A minute later as the St. Olaf center was shooting a free throw, Bowwow jumped up, hooked her thumbs under the straps of her bib overalls, and threw back her head.

"KILLLLLLLLLLL THA BASTUURRRRDDDDS!!!!!!!!!!!!!!!!!!!!"

This was definitely not in the repertoire of our high school cheers. There was a moment of total silence, but then Emil Hooper, the owner of the Red Owl Store, stood up with a bottle of Nesbitt's Orange in his hand. The pop in the bottle had darkened to a deep amber during the halftime break.

"YEAH! KILL THA BASTARDS!!!"

The crowd began to throb with a rhythmic chant.

"KILL—KILL—KILL—KILL…"

The St. Olaf players and coach looked wildly around at the sinister mob in the gymnasium—the building started to pulse with the cadence of the crowd. A concerned Arvi Swanson looked up at his truss.

Although our ranks were sadly depleted, the Iron Miners became a driven team. In a matter of minutes, we scored four straight baskets, putting us ahead by three points! Everybody in the gym was on their feet, screaming—metal chairs were kicked over—popcorn was flying everywhere. Guys were slugging down that curiously colored soda pop.

But in the process of reaching out to intercept a pass, Petersen fouled their center. It was his fifth foul—he was now out of the game.

O'Neal's shoulders sagged visibly, and he got up and looked at us three B-Squaders sitting on the bench. He pointed at Carl Kettu to go in for Petersen. We had a three-point lead, but there were still fifty seconds left on the clock, and we had just lost our main scoring and rebounding player. Anything could happen.

Sure enough, even though the St. Olaf center missed the free throw, one of their players picked up the rebound and took a shot. Missed. But they picked up the second rebound and finally scored the basket. With Petersen gone, there was no way we could get any rebounds. We still had a one-point lead, but if they ever got the ball again, they were sure to score the winning basket.

We got the ball down the court, and Mutt took a shot. It bounced off the rim, and in the scramble, Hanson touched it as it went out of bounds. St. Olaf now had the ball, with twenty seconds left on the clock.

The momentum had clearly shifted. Their coach had a wolfish grin on his face as he lit up his third cigar of the night. One of their guards brought the ball down the near sideline to go in for the final basket.

At the same moment, After-Shave got up from his chair.

At first it looked like he was going to step out on the court to intercept the St. Olaf guard, but he just stood there, teetering precariously close to the baseline but staying out of bounds. The blood was still flowing freely from the beer-bottle gash on his face. His eyes glowed like hot coals as he watched the St. Olaf guard approach with the ball. At the last second his dirt-and-blood-covered face broke into a satanic grin, the pinch of snuff slowly rolling out of his mouth and down his shirt front. The gargoyle from hell.

The St. Olaf guard made the mistake of locking eyes with After-Shave. He dribbled the ball off his own kneecap, and it sailed out of bounds.

The whole place went crazy. People slapped each other on the back—hunting caps went sailing in the air—more strange soda pop went down numbed gullets. There was still ten seconds left on the clock, but we had the ball and a one-point lead!

Just as suddenly, the place quieted down. Hake Hanson was sitting on the floor, holding his ankle and grimacing in pain. He was helped up and over to the bench. O'Neal turned and pointed at me.

Was he serious? Maybe he meant Rovaniemi, who was the only other player left on the bench. Questioningly, I pointed my finger at my chest and looked at O'Neal. He nodded. My heart went into my mouth, and my throat tightened up so badly that I couldn't swallow.

The Iron Miners called a time-out, and we clustered around the coach. I had grabbed the pine-tar bag we were using for our hands, squeezing it frantically. O'Neal put his hand on my shoulder. "Relax. You won't have to handle the ball at all. You're going to be the decoy when we put the ball in play. Hukala is the best ball-handler, so Kettu is going to look at you but fire a bounce pass to Hukala who'll be breaking in toward the sideline. All we have to do is get the ball in bounds and hang onto it for ten seconds." He looked down at my hands which were now the color of pipe tobacco from the pine tar. "An' for crissakes don't touch any of the St. Olaf players with those hands! You'll never be able to let go of him, an' we'll get a holding foul."

The referee blew the whistle, and we took our positions. All ten players were clustered in a tight group, the St. Olaf players, of course, trying to get possession of the ball. Kettu stood out of bounds, looked at me, and shot the bounce pass toward Mutt who was breaking in toward the sideline.

It's true what they say about the really terrifying things that happen to you; they do seem to occur in slow motion. The bounce pass went in toward Mutt as planned, but when it hit the floor, it struck one of the frost bumps and floated off at an oblique angle. Right toward me.

The basketball drifted up toward my chest, and I slowly put out my hands to grab it. But for some reason, all ten of my fingers were pointing straight out at the ball, and it hit my fingertips, the only part of my hands not covered with pine tar. The ball deflected off for parts unknown.

Players were milling around, slowly waving their arms, mouths open, and looking all around. Somebody stuck their foot between my legs, and I found myself toppling like a felled pine, heading for the floor.

As I was going down, I saw the ball ricocheting slowly off people's feet like it was in a dreamy pinball machine. Just as my body was about to hit the boards, the ball scooted in my direction and firmly wedged itself between my stomach and the floor.

Nine players landed on top of me, trying to get the ball, and I felt the basketball burrowing a hole in my stomach in quest of my spine. Somewhere, about a mile away, a whistle blew. Since nobody had managed to kick the brains out of my skull, I slowly realized that the game was over— we had won by one point.

With a shriek that went well past the range of the human ear, Bowwow leaped high into the frosty air, bounded over to After-Shave, and planted a kiss right on his lips.

After-Shave wasn't a virgin anymore.

A little more than a week later on a Sunday afternoon, three of us were sitting in a booth in the Bumblebee Cafe, and I was describing to Alice Maki how I had deftly snatched the ball away from the St. Olaf center and tucked it safely away as I was falling to the floor. Alice had been at the game but had caught an elbow in the eye, thrown in the heat of the moment by eighty-year-old Emily Keskitalo, and had missed the final seconds. Carl Kettu was sitting there nodding his head, silently verifying every word.

Carl had just taken a bite out of his cheeseburger when he looked over my shoulder at the front door. His mouth dropped open. "Jesuzzz! Kin that be who I think it is?"

Alice and I turned around and looked at a tall couple walking in—both of them looked vaguely familiar. Then it hit me.

Bowwow Bandini and After-Shave had just walked in...holding hands.

It couldn't be them—this guy wore clean clothes, had a fresh haircut, and blonde hair. After-Shave's hair was dirt brown and very long. This guy was clean-shaven and didn't have dirt tattooed in the lines in his face. But there it was—a half-healed, jagged scar on his right cheek. And the whites of his eyes were still pink around the edges. It was After-Shave all right—but it was the end of the month, and he was sober!!!

Bowwow's transformation was even spookier. Somebody had undone the bun and curled her hair. Her furry eyebrows had been plucked, and her eyelashes looked longer. She was wearing lipstick and...jesuzzz, her mustache was gone!

THEY HAD BOTH SHAVED!

Thelma Olson, the usually unflappable Bumblebee waitress, recognized them and dropped three orders of hamburgers, French fries, and Cokes on the floor. Everybody in the cafe was stunned at the metamorphosis.

Bowwow and After-Shave crammed themselves into a booth by the door, their bulk eclipsing the pale winter sunshine coming in through the front window. They looked intently into each other's eyes, oblivious to the stares.

Carl leaned over the table and reverently whispered, "Boy, jus' think about it—if those two got married and had a lotta kids, imagine what kind'a basketball team we'd have by 1967!"

Alice took a swig of Coke and answered dryly, "I hope they'll be making stronger basketballs by then."

The Loader

I stood in the middle of the bedroom in my BVD's—feet apart—arms locked in a duel—left hand clasped around the right wrist, pushing down mightily—right forearm resisting this force by pushing upward—my whole body vibrating like a tuning fork. Even my upper and lower teeth were clicking together like castanets.

Damn—it was really working! The veins in my forearms had popped up like blue snakes. My arms were definitely bigger than they were a couple of days ago.

I released the pressure, took a deep breath, and bent over the instruction book open on the bed. It prescribed three minutes for each arm—I had easily done that much. This wasn't so hard—in six months I'd have a magnificent, tough-as-nails, Charles Atlas body!

September 1948—I was pushing fifteen and a half, and my body was slugging it out with puberty—sprouting hair in the most interesting places, except on my chin where I really wanted it. But it was a well-known fact that regular shaving encouraged beard growth, so religiously every morning I scraped my face with the old man's Gillette razor, secure in the knowledge that the whiskers would wake up, sooner or later. However, the razor treated each new crop of pimples harshly, whacking them off with monotonous regularity. I used two yards of toilet paper every morning mopping up the damage.

In the last year I had sprouted up two and a half inches, certainly a welcome change since I no longer had to look up to enslave a girl with my cool, debonair stare. Unfortunately, my weight hadn't budged. When I posed in my underwear in front of our full-length mirror, I saw a Lake Superior shipwreck survivor who had spent two months on the water without fishing

*I stood in the middle of the bedroom in my BVD's—feet apart—
arms locked in a duel.*

tackle. Every rib visible—shoulder bones sticking out like epaulets—arms like plucked chicken wings. At five foot ten I weighed one hundred and forty pounds. It was a revolting sight.

Ah...but Charles Atlas had come to the rescue! I had seen his ads on the back pages of comic books for years, but being the chubby rascal that I was in my younger years, I had paid them no mind.

You know the ad—a skinny guy on the beach with this great-looking girl, as another guy, who could have easily played defensive line for the Chicago Bears, kicks sand in his face. The skinny guy objects, but being outweighed by a ton and a half, he's publicly humiliated and loses the girl in the process. So he sends away for Charles Atlas' secret for body-building, and get this, "months later" he's got a body like Joe Louis. He goes back to the beach, gets his girl back, and sends the sand-kicker packing.

The ad said that I could get a valuable, illustrated thirty-two-page book absolutely free! I would learn all about a new scientific method called "Dynamic Tension," which had already made over the bodies of thousands of other fellows, young and old—and it only took fifteen minutes a day! I cut the coupon from a comic book, put it in an envelope, and sent it off. I was desperate—around here, in the Upper Peninsula of Michigan, there were guys who would do a helluva lot more than kick sand in your face if you got on their bad side.

Three weeks later, the book finally arrived. For openers, it claimed to be only the *first* phase of the complete Charles Atlas program, and it described what amazing things the *second* phase would do for you. The second phase cost a dollar ninety-five, and Charles Atlas urged you to send for it immediately. Since I didn't have a dollar ninety-five, I continued to read. The book finally got around to describing a few basic exercises in "Dynamic Tension," which consisted of pushing one of your arms against the other for all you're worth. It didn't sound like much, but it did make the veins in my arms pop out, and it sure felt good when I stopped.

But the guy in the ad looked like he had put on about forty or fifty pounds along with his new muscles. Clearly, just pushing one arm against the other wasn't the whole answer. He must have shoveled in the chow pretty good to gain that much weight in a matter of months.

The obvious solution—try it both ways—keep up with the "Dynamic Tension" exercises and start eating more. For the last week, I had been piling in the food at every opportunity.

I went into the kitchen with my newly cultivated self-confident swagger. My mother, having noticed my new-found zest for eating, had cooked up a truly formidable supply of pancakes for breakfast. I sat down and loaded up my plate with two stacks of pancakes, five to a stack. The old man looked down at my plate with uneasy curiosity as he licked the edge of a Zig-Zag paper for his after-breakfast cigarette. The wheels were turning in his head, calculating how much money my breakfast was costing him.

"I don' know where yer puttin' it all. Did one a yer legs get hollow alluva sudden?"

"I dunno. Just hungry, I guess." I carved off an inch-thick slice from the pound of butter.

"Y'know ya ate a pound a butter yesterday?" He turned to my mother at the stove. "Why don'tcha buy oleo, it's cheaper."

"Oleo!" my mother snorted. "I'll never buy that junk again! It was bad enough we had to eat it during the war."

"I don' mean that *you an' me* should eat it. Jus' feed it to the kid, an' we'll eat the butter."

She wiped her hands on the dish towel. "Look, don't pester him about food. He's still growing."

"How much bigger you figger he's gonna get? Y'know that las' night he ate six pork chops? I can't afford t'buy pork chops at that rate! Mebbe we jus' oughta get ridda the middle man an' buy a herd a pigs."

I stayed out of the debate and forcibly crammed the last few forkfuls of pancakes into my mouth. He'd be sorry he said that when he saw my great-looking muscles next spring. Realizing that trying to constrain my daily nourishment was a no-win proposition, the old man changed the subject. "Ya pickin' out at Carlson's farm this year?"

"Yup," I replied.

For two weeks in September, most activities in many areas of the Upper Peninsula came to a halt while the potato crop was picked. This was urgent business since an early frost might put a blight on the crop. School was out, and every available able-bodied adult and kid went to the potato fields.

Picking potatoes was one of the few ways a kid could earn good spending money. If you were quick, you could pick between thirty or forty bushels a day, and at ten cents a bushel, this came to a lot of money in two weeks. Since I was saving up for my first car, I really needed the dough.

My stomach gurgled in revolt as I lurched from the table. With luck, the two-mile walk to Carlson's farm would settle my breakfast enough so I could bend over to pick the potatoes.

The tractor chugged by several rows to my right, pulling the two-row digger behind it. As a thick cloud of dust and exhaust fumes settled over me, I straightened up from picking to take a break. Potato picking wasn't easy work—while the digging machine clawed up the potato plants, exposing the potatoes growing on the roots, you still had to paw through heavy clods of dirt to make sure you got them all. But by nine o'clock in the morning I had already picked ten bushels, burning off most of my colossal breakfast. I poured myself a cup of coffee from my thermos bottle to celebrate my progress. I finished up the coffee just as Carlson's flatbed truck came down the rows to pick up the bagged potatoes. Old man Carlson's son, Donny, was at the wheel. While Donny had been a friend of mine for years, I was jealous as hell because his old man was totally unconcerned with minor details like the legal driving age in Michigan. Donny had been driving that truck since he was fourteen.

Carlson stopped the truck. "Hey, how'ya doin'?"

"Pretty good. Ten bushels so far."

"Yer gonna break my old man's bank."

I glanced at the two guys loading sacks on the truck. Pike Raskas grabbed the neck of a bushel sack with each hand and effortlessly swung them up onto the truck bed where Ducky Kangas stacked them up. "Don'cha usually have three loaders?"

"Yeah, but Frenchy tol' me yesterday he had t'help his uncle build a new shed, so it caught us shorthanded."

A bolt of inspiration hit me—loading paid much better than picking— I'd be able to sock away a lot of cash for the car, and it was perfect for my bodybuilding.

"Uh...how 'bout lettin' me take the loading job?"

Carlson gave me a diplomatic half-smile. "Ah...I don't think ya gotta 'nuf beef for the job."

"Whaddaya mean? I been workin' out—I got the reach an' a lotta energy. Gimme a try."

Carlson looked doubtful. "Well...lemme ask th'old man when we get back to the root cellar. I'll let ya know later."

My heart was thumping as I went back to picking. Gawd—a loader! Aside from the good pay and bodybuilding, it was a gigantic promotion in status. A loader in a potato field was like a lifeguard at the beach. Girls stopped their picking, smiled, and offered you a cold drink from their thermos bottles when you passed by. All of the loaders wore white, tight T-shirts to show off their muscles and had red or blue bandannas tied around their foreheads to keep the sweat out of their eyes—I just had to get that job!

An hour and a half later, Carlson pulled up in the truck and leaned out the window. "The old man didn't think too much of you being a loader, but he agreed to try ya out for a day or two to see how it goes. The pay is a buck an hour. Izzat OK?"

I had never made that much money in my life, but I clung to my composure, "Yeah, that's OK. When do I start?"

"Tomorrow. Be at the root cellar at nine. We don' hafta start till the pickers've bagged a truckload." He drove off.

Unbelievable! Not only was the pay better, but loaders worked bankers' hours!

The next morning I fished out an old, white T-shirt that had shrunk from washing. Hands on hips, I assumed a Charles Atlas stance in front of the mirror in my tight T-shirt and BVD's. I looked like a whippet trying out for a dog's basketball team. Oh, well...

I sat down at the kitchen table to a stupefying heap of scrambled eggs. "Wow! Lookit all these eggs!"

The old man was carefully pouring coffee into his saucer to cool it down. "Couldn't afford to buy 'em. Hadda knock over Mattila's henhouse this mornin'."

My mother ignored his twisted sense of humor. "You just sit there and eat. You're going to need lots of energy loading those potatoes."

The old man took a slurp from his saucer of coffee. "I dunno...I don' think ya weigh enough fer a job like that."

"Aw...I'll be OK. I'm stronger'n I look." The scrambled eggs were seriously stretching my stomach muscles. "Boy! I dunno if I can finish all these eggs. Mus' be a dozen or more on this plate."

"Would'a been more, but I hadda peg some a them at Mattila's dogs when they caught me in the henhouse," the old man said.

I got to the root cellar before nine. The root cellar, a long, low building half dug into a hill, was where old man Carlson stored the potatoes until they were shipped out. Donny Carlson and Ducky Kangas were already there. Ducky was a big, beefy kid with a thick neck and sloping shoulders—he didn't talk much but took orders well.

Hardly able to contain my excitement, I stood at the door of the root cellar, looking at the cavernous, dark interior. Suddenly, my right arm became paralyzed—I jerked my head around, coming face to face with Pike Raskas who had encircled my biceps with his gorilla-like hand. Pike was eighteen and had dropped out of school years ago for lack of talent and interest. He had a sloping forehead and wide-set, unblinking, yellow-green eyes under a thatch of muddy-brown hair. An oversized mouth housed pointed, rotting teeth that had never seen the inside of a dentist's office. While Pike had a natural flair for jobs requiring manual labor, he was also very good at rearranging your face if you caught him in a grumpy mood.

As Pike pulled me close, my right fingers went numb. Sour breath assaulted my nostrils as he spoke to me in a low, gutteral voice. "I gotta chunk a liver sausage in my lunch pail thet's got more muscle in it than yer arm. I know ya got this job cause yer buddy-buddy with ol' man Carlson's kid. Asked 'em t'give my brother Toad a loadin' job, an' they sez he's too young. Sheeet! He's fourteen, an' he could throw you over that flatbed truck without even raising a sweat! This is tough work, candy ass, an' ya better not fall down on the job, or I'll kick yer head in!" He let go of my arm and walked away.

My rapier-like wit put my tongue in gear. "Oh, yeah? Don' worry about me! I can handle this!" Nonchalantly, I flopped my right forearm against my leg to get the blood back into it.

Carlson got behind the wheel of the truck. "OK, jump on, an' let's get to work."

We rode on the bed of the truck out to the field where the pickers had already bagged two or three hundred bushels. Resplendent in my tight, white T-shirt and red bandanna, I waved at some of the girls I knew from school. They straightened up and stared at me, their mouths hanging open.

Pike and I started loading the sacks onto the truck, handing them up to Ducky, who was standing on the bed, stacking them in rows. Carlson would help load the sacks and then jump behind the wheel from time to time and move the truck.

It only took a half hour for the romance with the loading job to evaporate. A bushel sack of potatoes normally weighs between forty or fifty pounds, but old man Carlson, like all potato farmers, wanted his money's worth from the pickers, insisting that the sacks be chock full before they were tied shut. That meant that every twenty seconds or so, I was picking up fifty- or sixty-pound sacks of potatoes.

When Ducky had completely covered the truck bed with sacks, he jumped on top of them and started to stack on another layer. Now I had to lift the sacks about two feet higher.

Ducky looked down and snapped his fingers impatiently as I grunted and struggled to push a sack up to his outstretched fingers. "C'mon, c'mon, I ain't got a sky hook up here! Push 'em up t'me!"

My arms felt like lead, and I was developing a noticeable wobble as I plodded alongside the truck. Forehead sweat mixed with the dust made rivulets of mud that ran down my cheeks.

I couldn't believe my eyes! Ducky started on a third layer, meaning that I had to hoist the sack completely over my head for him to grab it. We were building a pyramid of potatoes on the back of the truck.

I was flirting with full cardiac arrest by the time Carlson decided that we had a full load and were ready to go back to the root cellar. Opening the passenger-side door of the truck, I put my right foot up on the door frame but didn't have enough strength to lift my depleted body into the truck. Pike came up behind me, put his hands on the seat of my pants, and disgustedly shoved me into the cab. He climbed in after me, and Carlson took off.

I sat there, in a petrified state, gazing blankly ahead through the dusty windshield. If Charles Atlas had to do this for a living, he wouldn't be talking about that "Dynamic Tension" crap.

Pike gave me a vicious jab to the ribs with his left elbow. "How d'ya like loadin'? Course, ya ain't seen the bes' part yet."

"Whaddaya mean?" I croaked.

"Who th'hell d'ya think unloads the truck? Little elves who live in the root cellar?"

"Gets pretty dusty in there," Carlson added.

Pike gave me a sinister leer. "Betcha ya thought we wore these bandannas jus' fer show."

Carlson drove the truck into the dark innards of the root cellar. There were huge bins on both sides, some of them, toward the back, full of potatoes but most still empty. Dim light bulbs hung from the ceiling. Carlson backed the truck up to one of the empty bins and killed the engine.

Pike jumped out of the truck, pulled the bandanna down from his forehead to cover his nose and mouth, and produced a jackknife from his pocket. He stepped into the empty bin just as Ducky threw a bushel of potatoes from the top of the load on the flatbed. Pike caught it, cut the cord from the mouth of the sack, and spread the potatoes across the bin.

Without thinking, I staggered into the bin and looked up at Ducky just as a sack of potatoes was coming right at me. With energy I didn't know I had left in me, I jumped aside.

WWHHUUUMMMPPP!!!

The sack hit the floor, broke open, and split potatoes scattered all around.

That was close! I was busy congratulating myself on narrowly escaping serious injury when Pike bellowed at me.

"YA THINK WE'RE MAKIN' GAWDAMNED MASHED POTATOES IN HERE? YER SUPPOS'TA KETCH THA SUNSABITCHES!"

Catch them! He must be joking—I could barely *lift* them!

Carlson stepped up to me. "Look...jus' go up to the truck, grab the sacks, an' carry 'em into the bin. Let Pike an' Ducky throw 'em."

So I lugged the sacks into the bin—and I lugged more sacks into the bin. Soon, the dust blotted out the light from the bulbs and the doorway. The bandanna over my nose didn't do much to help—the dust got in my eyes, ears, and throat. I couldn't breathe, and all I could see was dim outlines of people and potato sacks moving around. I could have been on some alien planet in a forced labor camp.

Carlson stopped the truck in front of my house, and with extreme effort, I painfully inched out of the cab. Like a ninety-year-old man, I took slow, small, unsteady steps up to the kitchen door. I couldn't have told you how many sacks of potatoes we had hauled to the root cellar that day, but if old man Carlson could deliver all those potatoes to the Marquette Airport and get them on the Berlin Airlift, he could have brought the Russians to their knees.

My mother looked at me as I gingerly stepped into the kitchen, and her hand flew up to her mouth. "What happened to you? How did you get so much dirt on you in only one day? Just stop right where you are! You're not coming into my clean house until you wash off that dirt!"

Like a whipped dog, I trailed her outside where she took the washtub from the outside wall of the woodshed and brought it over to the garden hose by the kitchen door.

"Take off those filthy clothes, get in the washtub, and hose yourself down. I'll bring you some clean things."

The final indignity of the day. I had to take a cold bath with a garden hose in the back yard, in plain sight of the neighbors.

My mother brought out clean clothes, a towel, and a bar of Fels-Naptha soap. I stripped down, turned on the hose, and climbed into the tub. The cold water clutched my heart, and every muscle in my body screwed up tight and screamed in agony.

Somehow I got through the bath, turning the tub water a dark, chocolate color. I struggled into the clean clothes and staggered into the kitchen. The old man was sitting at the table, drinking his tenth coffee of the day. My mother was putting the food on the table for supper. A big plate of fried Spam and...

A heaping bowl of MASHED POTATOES!

My stomach recoiled at the thought of eating potatoes, and I collapsed into my chair. "I ain't too hungry tonight."

"AIN'T HUNGRY?" they cried in unison.

I saw the old man's mouth angrily twitching as he mentally computed the cost of the food on the table, and I hurriedly scooped some potatoes on my plate. "Well, maybe just a plateful or two."

I was tied, hand and foot, to the railroad tracks, and the Lake Superior and Ishpeming locomotive, pulling one hundred fully-loaded, iron-ore cars, had just run over me. I could see the engineer, way down the track, looking back at me with a villainous grin. He stopped the train and started to back it up. He was going to run over me again—he was even ringing the bell to make sure that no one was on the track but me! As the train picked up speed in reverse, he rang the bell faster and faster...

I opened my eyes and stared at my bedroom ceiling. The old, brass alarm clock was clanging away on my dresser. I started to reach over to turn off the alarm—I couldn't move my arm. I tried to get out of bed—I couldn't move my legs. I was paralyzed.

My gawd! I had contracted polio overnight! Did my parents know? No, they didn't...I could hear my mother in the kitchen making breakfast, humming to herself.

Wait a minute—I could move my fingers. With supreme effort, I raised my right arm—it felt like it had a concrete cast on it. Very slowly, inch by inch, I sat up on the edge of the bed. There wasn't one square inch of my body that didn't hurt. Those five hundred thousand bushels of potatoes that I lifted yesterday were sitting on top of me.

With snail-like movements, I squirmed into my clothes. My snow-white T-shirt of yesterday now looked like I had been caught in the crossfire of an intense cow-turd fight. I glanced at the "Dynamic Tension" book sitting on my dresser, with Charles Atlas beaming confidently from the cover. *If you came here, Atlas, I could fix you up with a job that would wipe that silly grin off your face.*

I shuffled into the kitchen and gently lowered my mangled body into a chair at the table. My mother set down a plate in front of me.

Potato pancakes? *Potato* pancakes? Was this another nightmare? If it was, bring back the ore train—I could handle that better.

She saw the strangled look on my face. "Not hungry again? Well, I had to do something with the mashed potatoes you didn't eat last night! Eat!"

I walked the two hundred miles out to Carlson's farm. My arms and legs loosened up somewhat, but the walk took about ten minutes longer than it did the day before. Pike and Ducky were sitting on the back of the truck bed, waiting for me.

Pike lit up a Camel from a pack that he had rolled up in the sleeve of his T-shirt. He jerked his head toward me and let out a raspy chuckle. "Whaddaya think, Ducky? This guy don't look too perky this mornin'. Ya think he stayed up too late las' night, chasin' women?" Pike exposed his ragged teeth in a predatory grin. "Ya better move faster than ya did yesterday, lollipop, or I'll take half yer pay."

I rode out to the field in the truck cab with Carlson. Pike was in a playful mood, and he might decide to toss me off the back of the truck just for laughs.

I knew that the pickers had been out there since sunup, but I still couldn't believe the number of potatoes already bagged. Long columns of filled sacks stood waiting for us, like battalions of khaki-clad, headless, dumpy soldiers. Yesterday we had cleaned them out, but this morning another army had moved in...and tomorrow there'd be another...and the day after that, another. My puppylike biceps quivered in terror—I was going to be a casualty in the war of the potatoes.

After fifteen minutes of loading, my body sent a message to my brain...

Didn't you learn your lesson yesterday? Why don't we just go back home, have a nice lunch, and take a nap?

By the time Ducky started to put on the third layer, my arms were screaming in silent agony. The only way that I could get a sack to him was to lift it up and push it against the sacks already on the truck. Then, I'd bend over, get my head underneath the sack, hold it steady with both hands, and slowly straighten up. Ducky would take it off the top of my head.

I was slumped down, sitting in the middle, as we rode to the root cellar with the first load of the day. Carlson looked over at me. "How'r'ya holdin' up? Ya look pretty fagged out. Ya wanna quit now? Give ya a half a day's pay."

Pike lit up a Camel. "Ya better take that deal since ya won't last half a day. It ain't even ten a'clock, an' yer ass is draggin' in the dirt."

I pulled my bandanna over my nose as I sluggishly stepped into the root cellar bin next to the truck.

"HEY, POTATO-HEAD! CATCH!"

I looked up. Pike had jumped up on top of the load on the back of the truck. Since the bin I was in only had about a foot of potatoes in it, he towered over me, and he had a full sack in his hands. He swiveled his hips and launched the sack into the air.

The sack of potatoes arced high above my head, spinning like a hippopotamus doing a one-and-a-half gainer from a diving board. Pike had executed the throw perfectly. The sack plummeted down toward my head.

Another message from body to brain...

I told you an hour ago that we should have gone home!

This was it—my final exam in potato loading. If I caught this sack, it'd show them that I had what it takes to be a loader. I braced myself and put up my hands—I had to catch this sack!

WWHHHUUUMMMPPP!!!!!!!!

I didn't even slow it down—like a mosquito getting hit with a cannonball. The sack smashed me to the floor of the bin, flat on my back.

Pike cackled with glee when he saw that he had scored a direct hit. He grabbed a second sack and threw it at me...

WWWHHHUUUMMMPPP!!!!!!!

Then a third...WWWHHHUUUMMMPPP!!!!!!

Carlson ran up to the back of the truck, to get Pike to stop, but he was out of control. He was a human howitzer, launching potatoes at the enemy.

WWWHHHUUUMMMPPP!!!!
WWWHHHUUUMMMPPP!!!!

Potato sacks exploded all around as I lay there, half-buried and helpless. Have you ever wondered how you're going to die and what your funeral would be like? I had—and now I knew—I was going to die from terminal fatigue and be buried at sea—a sea of potatoes.

Water splashed in my face—I opened my eyes and saw Carlson standing over me with a water dipper in his hand. He gave me a sad smile.

"Ya know? I hate to say it, Jer, but I think ya oughta go back to pickin'."

The next morning I inched forward on my knees, scrabbling around in the dirt for the potatoes, since I was still too stiff and sore to bend over and pick. I had aged a lot in the last few days: from a dynamic fifteen-year-old, well on his way to a perfect Charles Atlas body, to one of the elders, on his knees in the field, painfully excavating the meager number of bushels that a worn-out body would allow.

Somebody gave me a heart-stopping slap on the back. Bolts of pain shot up and down my spine. I turned my head to look up at a somewhat diminished version of Pike Raskas, his younger brother Toad. He wore a clean, white T-shirt and a fresh, red bandanna tied around his head. His stupid, wide grin showed greenish, decaying teeth—not quite as bad as Pike's, but then he was four years younger. Last June, following in the foot-steps of his brother, Toad had loudly declared that he was done with school and was going to go out and start earning real money.

"I jus' wanna thank ya fer steppin' aside an' givin' me a chance to show my stuff. Ya feelin' better today, now that yer off the *heavy* work? Heh, heh, heh, heh, heh."

Pike came up alongside and put his hand on Toad's shoulder. They both grinned in unison...a dentist's fantasy.

"Ya shouldn'ta slapped 'im onna back so hard, Toad. He's feelin' sort'a delicate today."

The high-spirited pair ambled off, flipping sacks effortlessly onto the truck. With gritted teeth, I resumed pawing through the dirt. Revenge! I had to think of a way to get revenge!

Later on in the morning, the truck came by again for their second load. Toad's T-shirt had now taken on the hue of a freshly unearthed night crawler. His soggy bandanna was hanging limply around his neck, and...could it be true? Did I see him stagger a bit as he threw that last sack on the truck?

"How'ya doin', Toad? Pretty good job, huh?"

"I'm doin' fine. Jus' stick to yer pickin'!"

"Keep smiling, Toad. About three or four more truckloads, an' you'll be done for the day. Course, then, there's tomorrow, an' the day after, an' the day after that..."

Having that little conversation with Toad cheered me up immensely, and I started to whistle a happy tune as I inched forward on my knees.

"Aarrhh!" I cracked my right knee on a large rock in the dirt. Today we started picking in Carlson's east forty, and the ground was loaded with rocks. I grabbed the rock to throw it aside and hefted it in my hands. It was the size of a small football and must have weighed at least ten pounds.

Hmmm...heavy as hell, but small enough...

An evil smile cracked the dust on my face. I had an empty potato sack at my side. Like a revolutionary about to plant a bomb, I furtively looked around. Everybody had their head down, engrossed in their picking. I quickly placed the rock in the sack and filled the rest of it with potatoes. Every time I started on another bushel, there always seemed to be a ten- or fifteen-pound rock within arms reach.

If you think the sacks are feeling heavier now, Toad, wait till you come by on the next pass. Of course, an extra ten or fifteen pounds per bushel...that's nothing for a strong, young guy like you, Toad. Hell, in no time at all, you'll look just like Charles Atlas...except, maybe, for the teeth.

I was savoring a delectable daydream of visiting Toad, with him lying in traction in the Ishpeming Hospital while I adjusted the pulleys attached to his bed, when I heard footsteps behind me.

"Hi, do you mind if I pick alongside you here?"

I looked up into the face of a young goddess—a face with inch-long lashes over deep, dark, liquid eyes—a face with full, exquisite lips—a face I'd never seen before. She looked to be about my age—dark hair peeking out from underneath a kerchief on her head—a new plaid shirt and freshly washed blue jeans. She carried a metal lunch box with an unfamiliar high school emblem on it. It was obvious that she had never picked a potato in her life, but who cared?

My urbane, sophisticated personality was in the same stage of development as my biceps. "Aahhh...yeah...sure, why not?" Quickly, I got up off my knees. My body had suddenly experienced a divine and instantaneous healing.

"I'm afraid I don't know anything about picking potatoes. I've never done it before."

"Well, there's not much to..." I put the brakes on my tongue. "Well, there are some things you hafta know before you start. You want me to show you how to do it?"

"Oh, yes. I'd really appreciate it. I'm Cecille, Cecille Gillette. We just moved into town a few days ago, from Grand Rapids."

From the Lower Peninsula—a foreign woman! This chance encounter was taking on exotic overtones. If I was going to get a snappy dialogue going, I needed some caffeine.

I introduced myself. "Uh...would you like some coffee? I've gotta ther-mos."

"Oh, no, thanks. I don't drink coffee."

Doesn't drink coffee? Well, this still had possibilities. I poured myself a healthy slug of coffee and bolted it down.

I screwed the cap back on the thermos. "Uh...so, what grade are you in?"

"The tenth. I thought I was going to be in the ninth, but the school up here found out that I had already taken almost everything that they offer in the ninth grade, so I got to skip it."

Skip the ninth grade? I knew guys who had taken the ninth grade so many times they had majored in it.

"The tenth? Hey, what a coincidence. Me, too."

"What courses have you decided to take this year?"

The coffee was stimulating my creative thinking processes. "Oh, whatever I need to complete my science requirements. I'll probably be majoring in physics at the University of Michigan in a few years. Learning how to design atomic bombs...that sort'a thing. We gotta keep the Russians in line, y'know."

Her eyes widened. "Wow! What a coincidence! I want to go to Michigan, too! I'll probably major in biology. I really like school. I can't wait for this potato-picking season to be over so school can start."

"Yeah, it's too bad they can't pick 'em in August. I come out here to do my share so that school isn't going to be delayed any longer than neces-sary."

The flatbed was now coming back in the opposite direction. They just about had a full load, and Toad grunted audibly as he hoisted one of my "special" sacks high over his head so Ducky could grab it.

Cecille pointed at Toad, who was now lurching drunkenly alongside the truck. "Look at that poor fellow! That must be a terrible job!"

"Yeah, I tried it for awhile myself, but it wasn't much of a mental challenge." I casually picked up another rock and placed it in an empty sack. I figured that a couple more of my *special* bushels would be all that it would take to put Toad on the ropes.

She gave me a puzzled look. "Why did you put a rock in that sack?"

"This rock? Uh...well...it's an idea I worked out on my own. If you put a rock in the bottom of the sack, it keeps the full bushel from gettin' top-heavy and tipping over when it's on the truck. I try to help out the loaders in any way I can."

"Why, that's a wonderful idea! You're going to be good at physics. Have you told the other pickers about it?"

"Uh...no, most people don't appreciate original ideas. Uh...don't say anything about it to anybody, 'specially the guys loadin' the truck. They might get sore 'cause they didn't think of it themselves."

"OK, you're a very unselfish person. But, I know how you feel...I feel sorry for them, too."

That got my total attention—I stopped picking. "You feel sorry...for the loaders?"

"Well...yes. Just look at them...bulging with muscles."

I straightened up suddenly, a potato in both hands, not believing what I had just heard. "You feel sorry for them because they got muscles?"

"Yes. You see, what I figure is that any guy who's got that kind of build has been doing manual labor for a long time. Maybe he had to quit school to help support his family...or maybe he just wasn't smart enough to get through. Whatever it is, he'll probably have to miss out on a lot of the best things in life."

A message from body to brain...

Are you listening to this? Throw the Charles Atlas book in the stove! I'll never be a mountain of muscle anyway—look at your old man. That's what I'm gonna look like in thirty years, no matter what you do. Use your brains and quit bothering me with this "Dynamic Tension" crap!

I dropped both potatoes on the ground and started to chuckle.

"What's so funny?"

"Oh...I dunno...I just never thought of it that way before."

I looked down the row toward the truck. Heat waves shimmered off the top of the cab as Ducky was putting the last few sacks on the third tier. Toad was stumbling along with his shoulders slumped. His soaking-wet T-shirt was now a pasty, milk chocolate color. His feet were obscured in a cloud of dust. I leaned over and took the rock out of the burlap sack.

"I thought you just said that the rock was a good idea."

"Yeah, but I think it's about time those guys started to think of their own good ideas, don't you?" I walked over and picked up my lunch pail. "You wanna have lunch? I'll trade you some potato pancakes for *anything* in your lunch box."

First Date

I savored the dregs of my after-dinner coffee, gazing out at the serene panoramic view from the living room window of Carl and Elaine Kettu's sprawling ranch-style house overlooking the Michigamme River.

"Fantastic! You two been married almost *forty* years now." I wore a congenial smile, but inwardly I shivered, thinking what it would be like to have my ear drums lacerated by Elaine's buzz-saw tongue for forty years. Carl Kettu and I had been teen-age cronies and against the better judgement of some faculty members, had secured high-school diplomas together in the small, Upper Michigan mining town of Republic.

Elaine brought in a fresh pot of her Swedish gourmet coffee and refilled my cup. "Only forty years?" she asked dryly. "Seems longer."

Carl had assumed his usual slouch in the easy chair, stocking feet up on the ottoman. Popping the tab on another can of Old Milwaukee, he belched and shot an irritable scowl at his wife. "Whaddaya mean by that crack? We had some good years, didn' we?"

"Yeah...I guess so," she admitted. "I remember that 1954 and '55 weren't too bad."

The conversation was taking a decidedly ugly turn, so I put a gentle hand on Elaine's shoulder and said lightheartedly, "Hey, you remember that very first date you had with Carl?"

Elaine's eyebrows shot up. "Does Nixon remember the Watergate break-in? I can't imagine what I was thinking of when I agreed to go out with him. I must'a been struck blind by the dazzle of that new car. He's done a lotta stupid things in his day, but that date..."

I took a sip of fresh coffee while she babbled on, my mind nimbly racing back to a time when dates and cars were the center of my universe...

Taking a slow, deep breath, I let my brain mull over the delicious smell, but it was hard to pinpoint: a subtle blend of new rubber, fresh paint, and wax combined with an elusive fragrance impregnated in the velvety, pearl-gray cloth covering the seats, door panels, and overhead liner. Henry Ford must have had some top-secret scent sprayed into the cloth, one designed to dissolve the purse strings of even the most cautious new-car buyer.

Carl Kettu had just glided up to our house in a shiny, brand-new '49 Ford, and I was sitting behind the wheel. An inverted image of our battered woodshed shimmered in the black, mirror-like finish of the hood.

"No bull—is it really yours?"

"Naw, I stole it from some tourists who stopped along the highway to pick blueberries. A'course it's mine! I picked it up at Hooper's this mornin'."

I was a member of the mob that had invaded the tiny showroom of Hooper's Ford Agency last fall when the first '49 Ford was delivered. Everybody had to see the radical new design. The car didn't have any fenders—the side of the chassis was completely smooth from headlight to taillight! Not everyone had a positive reaction to this innovation. Why would anybody want such a car? some guys asked. How could you haul your buck out of the woods with a car that didn't have fenders? Others argued that anyone who would tie a bloody deer carcass to an automobile priced at over two thousand dollars should undergo immediate psychiatric examination. As far as I was concerned, these debates were on the same cosmic level as the origin of the universe, since I never in my life would be able to afford such a machine. But now Carl had one, and a bilious green lump of envy lodged heavily in my throat.

"Where the hell did'ya get the money?"

Carl fastidiously wetted the corner of a red bandanna with his tongue, knelt down, and scrubbed off a grasshopper that had the impudence to get himself squashed on the treads of one of the new whitewalls. "Don' ferget I been workin' on the old man's potato farm the last four years. Besides, I only had'ta put up a down payment. I'll be punchin' potato sacks fer the next fifteen years to pay 'er off. Right now, I don' even have 'nough money left t'put gas in it."

"You gonna cruise around tonight?"

"I jus' asked Elaine Olsen out, an' I thought maybe me an' Elaine an' you n' Alice could double date tonight."

"Jeez, that Elaine's a real looker, but how are ya gonna take out a new girl if yer broke? I don' have any dough either."

Carl dismissed our defunct financial condition with a shake of his head. "You don' hafta spend money to show a girl a good time." With a conniving smile he said, "I got'n idea fer tonight that won't cost us a dime—trust me."

I composed a mental image of Alice Maki reacting to a date that didn't involve the expenditure of money—it wasn't pleasant to look at—but the temptation of riding in Carl's new car was overwhelming.

"OK, I'll ask her."

Alice's eyes widened as she stuck her head in the open passenger-side door. She let out a low whistle.

"Jeez...whose car is it?"

"It's mine," Carl said.

"No—no kiddin'—whose car is it?"

"Dammit, it's really mine."

She looked at Elaine, sitting next to Carl. "Whose car is it, really?"

Elaine laughed, "It's really his," she said, pulling the back of her seat forward to let Alice get in the back, next to me.

Alice looked in at me and said, "Well, big spender, when're *you* gonna get one of these?"

With my voice dripping with indifference, I said, "Jus' get in th'car, will'ya?"

At nine o'clock it was just getting dusk and choruses of crickets were tuning up for the warm July night. We cruised slowly downtown from Alice's house, past the Spruce Grove Tavern, the bowling alley, and the Lutheran Church, down Fire Street, over to Kloman, and back downtown again. Although Hooper had sold several '49 Fords by now, pedestrians still stopped in their tracks and gawked at the fenderless car as we went by.

We had made this same loop three times when Elaine finally said to Carl, "Aren't we gonna do anything else besides circle around town? I'm starting to get dizzy."

"Yeah, but I'm waitin' for it to get dark."

At nine-thirty we were next to the firehouse at the bottom of the Fire Street hill. With no explanation, Carl pulled up behind a parked '38 Chevrolet and stopped. There weren't many street lights on Fire Street, and the one by the firehouse was burned out, so when he shut off the engine and turned off the headlights, we were in total darkness.

Elaine's voice snapped out of the blackness. "Is this the start of our date?"

Alice hissed in my ear. "I tol' Elaine that she better be careful, cause all he ever thinks about is you know what."

"Re...lax," Carl said, getting out of the car, "We're almost outta gas, an' I'm gonna show ya Kettu's economy, help-yourself service station." He went around to the back of the Ford and opened the trunk. I heard the muffled clatter of an empty gallon can, and I realized what was going on.

"What's he up to?" Elaine asked.

My eyes were getting adjusted to the darkness, and looking through the windshield, I saw Carl walk over to the rear of the parked Chevy. He stuck a rubber hose in the gas tank and put the other end in his mouth. "Uh...I think he's gonna siphon some gas outta that Chevy."

Siphoning gas out of other people's cars, a poor man's way of meeting automobile operating expenses, was an acquired taste in the literal sense of the word. You had to have a robust palate, since it required sucking the gas up through the hose to get the process started, and the criteria for success was getting a mouthful of gasoline. Aside from the fact that it was slightly illegal, this was the main reason that I never became much of a hand at siphoning, having tried it once and finding that I had trouble keeping food down for about a week afterwards. Nevertheless, it was a popular topic of discussion among the local delinquents who hung around Chub Mattila's Standard Station. Veteran siphoners like Pike Raskas maintained that they could easily tell the difference between the taste of regular and ethyl gasoline; furthermore, Pike claimed he siphoned gas out of old man Saari's Buick only, since Saari always used ethyl and Pike preferred the smoother taste.

Alice leaned forward, putting her elbows on the top of the front seat to get a better look. "You mean he's stealing gas?"

"Yup," I said.

"But...doesn't he know whose car that is?"

"Sure, it's Cliff Alatalo's."

"Not anymore," Alice replied, "Cliff sold it to Felix Arquette last week. Why d'ya think it's parked by Felix's house?"

All the saliva in my mouth evaporated. Felix Arquette was the last guy in town you would want to steal gas from, or anything else for that matter. He was the Chief of the town's Volunteer Fire Department and part-time Constable—strapping on a nightstick and an ancient .45 revolver to patrol the downtown area on weekends, when the three bars bulged with rambunctious lumberjacks. We didn't have a jail, so Felix dispensed justice right on the spot with his trusty nightstick. He was a hulking, hairy, ill-tempered guy, and if you could imagine a pissed-off black bear dressed in a plaid shirt and work pants and standing on his hind legs, you pretty much had a good likeness of Felix Arquette.

Carl had filled the gallon can and was unscrewing the gas cap on the Ford. I rolled down the rear window and whispered hoarsely, "Carl, that Chevy belongs to Felix now...let's get the hell outta here!"

Carl produced a funnel and poured the gas into the Ford. "Felix's Chevy, huh? Don' worry...he's downtown bustin' up drunks with his billy club. He won't be home till the bars close. Gonna fill the can up once more an' we're on our way."

He walked over to siphon another gallon out of the Chevy. I sat there twiddling my thumbs while the sweat rolled down my rib cage.

Alice poked Elaine on the shoulder. "I figure anybody who has to steal gas t'keep their car running isn't gonna be able t'manage the cost of a cheeseburger over at the Bumblebee Cafe. Whaddaya say you an' I get out and walk over there an' leave these two delinquents to pursue their life of crime?"

Elaine reached for the door handle. "Sounds like a good idea to me."

The three of us in the car heard it simultaneously—a distant clop-clop-clop-clop—getting closer—somebody running. Squinting my eyes, I stared at the streetlight about one hundred yards up the hill towards downtown. A runner plunged into the pool of light cast from the streetlight—a galloping black bear wearing a nightstick and a .45 revolver.

It was Felix, and he was coming right at us.

EEEEEIIIIIGGGGGGHHHHH!!!!!

I had never participated in harmonized screaming before—Alice, soprano; Elaine, alto; and while I was normally a baritone, abject panic drove me up to a tenor. I stuck my head out of the window and squealed at Carl.

"IT'S FELIX!!!!!!"

Carl had been standing at the rear of the Chevy, his lips wrapped around the end of the hose and his cheeks sucked in to get the siphoning started. Felix's name hit his ear drums at the same instant that the gasoline gushed into his mouth, and he swallowed a mouthful. He dropped the hose and the can and lurched back to the Ford, making a curious "urk-urk-urk" sound, like a seal that had just swallowed a bad fish.

He pounced behind the wheel, started the engine, and snapped on the headlights, lighting up Felix, who was attacking the Ford like a charging rhino. Carl slammed it into reverse, and the spinning rear wheels thundered gravel up on the bottom of the chassis.

"Whaddaya turn the lights on for?" Elaine bellowed.

"T'blind 'im."

"Then give 'im the high beams!"

"Yeah, good idea!" Carl's left foot slapped the dimmer switch by the clutch petal, hitting Felix's ugly face full force with the bright lights.

I was on a double date with Bonnie and Clyde.

When Felix saw the Ford start to back up, he summoned up a burst of speed that closed the distance between him and the front of the car to fifteen feet. With the upward cast of light from the headlights, he looked like James Cagney's meaner brother.

Felix's name hit his ear drums at the same instant that the gasoline gushed into his mouth, and he swallowed a mouthful.

Carl twisted his head around, looking out the back window to steer. Elaine, Alice, and I scrunched down in the seats to minimize the chance of Felix recognizing us. My sweaty palms were leaving paw prints on the new upholstery.

From low in the front seat, Elaine barked at Carl. "If you hadda siphon gas, why didn' ya do it earlier instead a draggin' the rest of us into it?"

"I only got the car this mornin'," Carl said, blowing bubbles of gasoline through pursed lips.

"My dad's gonna kill me for gettin' mixed up in this," Alice squeaked from the shadows behind the front seat.

"Felix'll save him the trouble if he catches us," I volunteered, as I braced for the impact of .45 slugs.

"Whaddaya think he'll do?"

"If he doesn't shoot us? Probably rip off the front bumper an' beat us to death with it."

As the Ford careened up the hill in reverse, Felix kept up with us for several seconds, his stumpy thighs working like pistons. But the hill finally took its toll on his stamina, and by the time we reached the top, he had stopped and was standing in the middle of Fire Street with his hands on his hips, panting, and cursing.

Tentatively, Elaine stuck her nose over the dashboard. "For a new car, this thing sure doesn't go very fast in reverse."

Carl backed up the car for another block or so, then swung it around, and we sped off into the darkness. He slapped the steering wheel in frustration. "Damn—damn—damn!"

I dried my palms on my pant legs. "What's the matter—you think he knows who we are?"

"Naw—we blinded 'im pretty good with the lights—but it'll take me weeks t'find another piece of rubber tubing like that!"

Alice, who had been down on the floor behind the front seat, got back up on the seat and straightened her clothes. "Just drop me off at the Bumblebee Cafe. This date just got a little too spicy for my taste...besides, I have to go to the toilet."

"I think I went on the car seat back there," Elaine added. Just lemme out with Alice."

Carl was having none of it. "Hey, c'mon...I'm really sorry 'bout that, but I got all kinds a stuff in the trunk for a picnic."

"A picnic...at night?"

"Yeah, it'll be fun, you'll see."

Carl drove a couple of miles south of town to Swanson's potato farm where we pulled off the main road onto a two-rut lane that skirted the east forty of the farm. As we neared the far end of the field, he stopped and killed the engine. Through the windshield, a stand of poplar trees were barely visible in the dim light cast by the pale half-moon.

"This is the picnic site?" Elaine asked.

Carl opened the door and got out. "Yup—lemme get the stuff outta the trunk."

Elaine swiveled her head around, looking out all the windows. "A thousand lakes within two miles of town, and he picks a potato field for a picnic?"

I stared at the dark mass of poplar trees standing one hundred yards in front of the car, and then it occurred to me what the reason might be for Carl picking this spot for his picnic. Naw...I thought...even *he* had more sense than to pull something like that on a date—especially a first date. But the thought was so outrageous that I couldn't get it out of my mind.

Carl opened the passenger-side door with a brown paper shopping bag in his hand. "Elaine, why don'cha slide over behind the wheel, an' I'll sit on this side. I'm bigger, an' it gives me more room."

Oh, jeez, I thought—my hunch was right! He's right-handed, and he wants to sit on the right side! Alice'll think I'm in on this and never speak to me again!

Elaine took a couple of Mason jars filled with colored liquids out of the shopping bag. "What's this?"

"Kool-Aid," Carl answered, "I got orange and raspberry. There's some Twinkies in there, too. I brung four straws—we'll pass the jars around, an' everybody jus' puts their straw in an' sucks up."

Alice gave me an accusatory look, no doubt thinking that I had masterminded the catering. "We're having a picnic at night, next to a potato field, with Twinkies, Kool-Aid in jars, and straws?"

Elaine pulled another Mason jar out of the bag, filled with a yellow-ish liquid. "What flavor is this?"

"Don' drink that!" Carl hastily interjected, "That's the mosquito repellant."

She unscrewed the cap and put it up to her nose.

"GAAAAAAAAAAAAGGGGGGGGHHHHHHHHHH!!!"

Scrunching up her nose and squeezing her eyes shut, she slapped the cap back on the jar. "What's in it?"

Carl dipped two fingers into the jar and started to rub the liquid on his face and ears. "It's my own invention, an' it really works—it's kerosene, vinegar, a li'l turpentine, with some linseed oil t'keep yer skin from dryin' out."

As if on cue to accept the challenge, a squadron of mosquitoes roared in through the open windows of the Ford. Upper Peninsula mosquitoes were normally classified as dangerous carnivores, but that year we had an unusually wet spring and the surrounding lakes and cedar swamps were filled with standing water. The resulting mosquitoes were enormous—the big multi-engine variety that carried small animals off into the swamps.

WWHHAAAAAPP!!!!

My skull rebounded off the back of the seat as Alice smacked my forehead with a looping left hand. "Mosquito on your forehead," she said smugly.

SSMMAAAACCKK!!!!!

I countered with a lightning right jab that caught two of them ready to drill into her left biceps.

Swatting your date's mosquitoes was Upper Michigan's prelude to necking and petting. It afforded immediate physical contact that didn't require a lot of artfulness. Putting your hand on a girl's knee, or other places, was a test in timing, subtlety, and charm, so biffing her in the ear to nail a mosquito was an excellent preliminary. I was weighing the pros and cons of going after a mosquito that had gotten hopelessly entangled in the fuzzy wool on the front of Alice's angora sweater when Carl broke this erotic interlude by passing back the Twinkies and the Mason jars of Kool-Aid.

We sat there for the next several minutes, solemnly munching the Twinkies and sipping the Kool-Aid. Carl's homemade repellant worked great, keeping the mosquitoes buzzing around his head at bay. Unfortunately, it also repelled women—Elaine moved all the way over to the left side of the front seat.

Carl looked down at his half-eaten Twinkie. "These Twinkies taste strange to you?"

"Everything must taste strange to somebody who goes around sucking gasoline out'a people's cars," Elaine replied.

Carl stopped in mid-chew and put up his hand. "Shhhh!" He stared intently out of the windshield towards the poplar trees.

"Whaddizzit? What's out there?" Alice whispered.

Without taking his eyes off the trees, Carl slowly reached down beneath the front seat and brought out a 30-30 carbine. He eased the barrel out of the window.

Elaine stared at the rifle like it was a snake. "Whaddaya gonna do? Izzit a bear out there? Let's jus' get out'a here!"

"I think I hafta go to the toilet" Alice said.

Carl had the 30-30 pointed at the poplar trees. I leaned forward and whispered. "Don' forget t'jack a shell into the chamber."

"Did that at home. Makes too much noise out here."

Elaine straightened up indignantly. "Y'mean to tell me I've been sittin' on top of a rifle that could've gone off?"

"Relax, I had the safety on." Carl sighted down the barrel. "Turn on the headlights."

Tentatively, Elaine pulled the headlight knob. The grove of poplar trees lit up in a blaze of light. Standing motionless in front of the trees, eyes glowing like coals, and hypnotized by the headlights, was a doe.

Carl cocked the hammer of the 30-30 and took aim.

"IT'S A DOE!" Elaine yelled.

The scream broke the deer's spell, and it dashed into the trees. Carl pulled the trigger.

KAAA...POWWWWWW!!!!!!

The blast reverberated around the inside of the car, blocking my ears. Elaine kept yelling. "That was a *doe*! Didn'cha see it didn't have any horns?"

Carl kept looking at the trees and levered another shell into the chamber. "A'course it wuz a doe! They make the best eatin'—meat's nice'n tender. I don' think I got 'er though—she bolted too quick. Why'ja yell like that for?"

"You can't shoot does! It's illegal!"

Carl was now getting irritated. "A'*course* it's illegal! Wadda'ya think shooting 'em at night, using headlights, is?"

"They don't like it when you shoot 'em in July, either," Alice added.

Carl got out of the Ford. "Gonna go over an' see if I hit it." He started plodding through the potato field towards the trees.

Elaine gave us a stricken look. "He didn't hit it, did he? Gawd, I hope not!" She got out of the Ford. "I gotta find out if he hit it!"

Alice and I got out and followed her to where Carl was standing at the edge of the trees. He was poking at a light-colored object lying in the grass at the edge of the potato field.

"What's that?" Elaine asked.

"A salt lick. I put 'er there a coupla months ago. It attracts the deer."

"You mean...you knew that deer was gonna be here tonight?"

"Figured there wuz a pretty good chance there'd be one or two here."

Elaine put her hands on her hips. "So this...this picnic you arranged...you brought us out here to this hellish, mosquito-infested potato field to see if you could shoot a deer."

"Hey, whaddaya bellyachin' about? I wuz gonna split up the deer fair an' square between us!"

Elaine's voice now dripped with sarcasm. "Oh! Thank you very much! Some guys bring their dates flowers—I get the hind end of a deer!"

"Well, you would'a if you'd kept your mouth shut back there in the car."

Just then, the poplar trees lit up with light—headlights. Somebody was coming along the road.

Carl dashed back to the Ford, doused the headlights, and ran back. "Get down!" he snapped. Without waiting for a response, he grabbed Elaine by the back of the neck and pushed her face-first into the dirt. Alice and I ducked down.

But, the car kept on going and was soon out of sight. Carl got up slowly. "Could'a been Tikkanen, the game warden. Ya can't be too careful." He looked down at Elaine, who was slowly getting to her knees. "Sorry bout that, but with that white blouse you got on, you're too easy to spot in the dark. That's why I bought a black car, y'know."

Elaine looked down at her blouse, which was now liberally embroidered with clods of dirt. "Look...look what you've done...I'm a mess!"

"Aw, that's nuthin' but dry dirt. It'll come right off." Carl reached over and began to vigorously brush off the front of Elaine's blouse.

Elaine wound up and slugged him in the left ear.

"KEEP YOUR HANDS OFF ME!"

"I told you he's nothin' but a sex fiend," Alice said.

Carl rubbed his ear. "Fer crissake, I'm jus' trying t'help. Look, tha next time we have a date, jus' wear somethin' dark."

Elaine's mouth fell open. "The next time we have a date? The next time we have a date? THERE ISN'T GONNA BE A GAWDAMNED NEXT TIME! YOU HEAR ME?"

Alice led Elaine away by the arm. "C'mon, we can walk back t'town, an' you can cool off. You don't wanna be using that kind of language in front of your mother when you get home."

The laughter subsided and Carl and I both wiped the tears from our eyes. Carl fished out his red bandanna and blew his nose. "Boy, we hadn't thought about that first date in years, hey, hon?"

Our reminiscence had also stirred an emotional response in Elaine. She had taken on an unusual, somewhat alluring demeanor as she stood there staring at Carl, fists clenched, trembling slightly all over with tiny flecks of foam at the corners of her mouth. I know some guys are turned on by women who have a penchant for violence, but personally, they make me nervous, so I quickly finished off my coffee and got up. "Well, it's been fun bringing back the old memories, but I've got an early morning planned, so I better be going."

Carl walked me out to my car in his driveway. I couldn't help staring at his '92 Ford in the garage. You don't see many black cars these days.

"Ya know?" he said, "I wuz jus' thinkin'...our fortieth wedding anniversary is comin' up, an' wouldn' it be fun...even kinda romantic, if I took Elaine out to that potato field, instead'a some fancy restaurant in Marquette. Like a surprise party, but only the two of us. I could mix up a batch of Kool Aid, bring some Twinkies...even whomp up some a that mosquito repellant. Mebbe even shove 'er down in th'dirt an' wrestle around a li'l, heh, heh, heh..."

I got in the car. "Yeah, well...good luck with that idea, Carl...but one word of advice. Leave the rifle at home. She might get to it first."

Biography

Jerry Harju was born in Ishpeming, Michigan, in 1933. During World War II his family moved to Milwaukee for a few years. After the war they moved back to Michigan's Upper Peninsula where Jerry finished grammar and high school in Republic. He went to Ann Arbor and got an engineering degree at the University of Michigan in 1957. After taking early retirement from the aerospace industry in California, Jerry now spends his time writing and travelling. His latest adventure was leading a tour of the High Arctic, including the North Pole. Jerry returns frequently to the Upper Peninsula to visit relatives and old friends and to roam through the woods where he hunted, trapped, and fished as a boy.

PLEASE RETURN TO:

Avery
COLOR STUDIOS

P.O. Box 308
Marquette MI 49855

CALL TOLL FREE
1-800-722-9925

Your complete shipping address:

_____
_____
_____
                        _____

Fold, Staple, Affix Stamp and Mail

_____
_____
_____

Avery
COLOR STUDIOS

P.O. Box 308
Marquette MI 49855